Something Twisted

Sarah Dale

Snowy Wings PUBLISHING

To Ellie and Harmony, for their excellent advice and their willingness to play along.

Printed in the United States of America

This edition Printed, 2021

ISBN-13: 978-1-952667-26-8
AISN: 978-1-952667-25-1

If you're reading this, you've found my hidey hole. I've been keeping journals of our adventures for more than three decades now, and up until last week, I believed them to be safely hidden in my home. Now, everything has changed.

It's not that I fear they will be discovered; rather the opposite. I fear they'll be destroyed, and the record of our life's work would simply disappear.

I'm putting them here for safekeeping. I've spent enough hours in this library to know what gets tended regularly, and what gets regularly overlooked. So if you're finding this now, you must be doing a deep clean. Or maybe, just maybe, the City has come together with the funds for a new building, and this one is being cleared out.

Do me a favor. Do what you can to keep these safe. Tuck them back away, or move them if you need to, but don't let them be destroyed.

And if it's you they're meant for, then, good luck, my friend. You're going to need it.

Preface

IT WAS NEARLY four years ago that we did pitched battle with Mitch, the almost-dead, still-a-jackass rotten boyfriend who wrecked David's mom's car and put her into a long-term health care facility. Since then, we'd learned and done an awful lot of real weird, real-life lessons. We'd learned that ghosts could get called back into the world and bring a taste of Hell with them; that not all ghosts are bad guys and sometimes the living are the absolute worst; and that our planet, and our species was far from alone in the universe. We'd learned that my Dad was in charge of guarding something called a Portal and that we—Jen, David and I—had been called to wield the power of the Triad to help him with his task.

Along the way we figured out that the slightly odd Vietnam War veteran, Mr. Rakow, who'd lived next door to David, was way cooler and more badass than we'd suspected, and that Jen and Jon's mom was a freaking amazing Witch and mine was a Master Healer. Jen, David and I had endured some boot-camp-like training to determine the extent of our powers as wielders of the Triad, among which were Jen's ability to see into the future, and my skills with magical healing.

Two years ago, we'd been transported to another planet to help Maka, the Grandmother and a young soldier named Malinowski save our friend Barb and her German Shepherd Alesta from Sa'uel who was the leader of a group of Pilgrims who were looking for a place they called Paradise. If you asked a Pilgrim what Paradise was, you were likely to be spun a tale of eternal peace and joy.

If you asked Maka or my dad, you'd get a different story; one that hinged on the scientific knowledge that this "Paradise" they sought was a galaxy-sized imbalance in the Force, to use a *Star Wars* analogy.

Paradise was a place at the very center of all the multiple universes, a holdover from the very beginnings, and it sucked in energy and matter, an action which balanced the creation of energy and matter in other places. If it was fed more than its delicate allotment of matter, say like hundreds of millions of damn-fool pilgrims looking for "Paradise" it could tilt the balance of the universe away from the matter-we-all-need-to-exist end, to the more giant-gaping-black-hole-of-nothingness end of the cosmic scale.

Not to mention the fact that the Pilgrims were so intent on finding the doorway to their Paradise that they'd been known to decimate the populations of entire planets just to find clues to its location. Malinowski was the sole survivor of one such scorched earth attack. Maka had found him there, too late to save his moon and his family from the Pilgrims, but in time to rescue him.

Although she hadn't even known it at the time, Barb was in possession of one of those clues. At one point during her time at Whitehall, the neighborhood group home for troubled kids, she'd snuck into the basement to hide from a staff person bent on disciplining her for a fight she'd started with another kid. In that dingy basement room, she'd stumbled upon some old black and white photos and a hand-scored musical journal written by a Wesleyan University Music teacher named Clara Mills, dated March of 1940.

Clara had died of seemingly natural causes in her office in the Music Building on the Wesleyan campus in April of that same year. That would be the C.C. White

Music Building, named for and constructed by the same C.C. White whose home was later donated to the city and had become the "White Hall for Troubled Youth." Twenty-three years after Clara's death, her ghost was spotted in the building. The story goes that a woman named Coleen Buterbaugh saw Mills' ghost in the same office where she had died. More specifically though, in Coleen's story, she looked out the windows of Clara Mills' office and saw a landscape unlike the one of the then present-day campus.

Buterbaugh, and later paranormal researchers took that to mean she was seeing the past, the way the campus would have looked in the 1940s when Clara Mills died. One inquisitive student, present on campus in the early 1960s, discovered something even more curious and disturbing. That student was my dad.

"IT WAS A weekend, so there weren't many folks on campus. I'd been in the library studying for an exam, and I cut through the Music Building on my way back to the parking lot." Dad told us the story one night. We were gathered around the kitchen table after supper on a Saturday. My sister Mallory was prone to skipping out of our weekly homemade pizza night early to go hang out with her friends, which made it the perfect time for the rest of us to gather and talk about things. Mal wasn't completely out of the loop, Mom and Dad had agreed that would be foolhardy. But she was encouraged to do her own thing, safe in the knowledge that that hard work of keeping the universe safe was being done by the rest of us.

Mom and Mr. Rakow were clearing the table and putting away leftovers. Jen and Lorraine were loading the dishwasher and David, Jon and I were busting out the after-supper cookies while dad made decaf.

"That was the day I met Maka for the first time," dad recollected, measuring coffee grounds into the basket. "And Clara Mills' ghost. I was walking, quite deliberately, I assure you," he grinned, looking around at us mischievously, "past Clara Mills' old office. I wasn't the only one who did it. Everyone on campus knew about the ghost. Stories like that travel like wildfire. Lots of students, and probably staff, too, would deliberately walk down that hallway, hoping to catch a glimpse of something supernatural. That afternoon, I sure got my wish!" He chuckled and carefully poured water from the carafe into the coffee maker.

"What did you see?" I asked.

"I saw Maka, seated cross-legged on the desk and Clara Mills' ghost standing, facing her directly. They were about three feet apart. There were no words being spoken out loud, but I could tell that both women were clearly deeply focused and reacting to one another, like there was a conversation happening that I just wasn't privy to. Neither of them noticed me in the doorway. I stopped dead in my tracks, fascinated. I couldn't tell if Maka was a hippie or a shaman. And Clara, oh my goodness. I could see through her just as plainly as I could see her standing there. I'm sure I looked like a complete fool with my eyes wide and my mouth agape. I'm just lucky I felt a blast of cold air just then, because it made me look at the windows."

"What was happening at the windows?" Lorraine asked, wiping her hands on a dish towel and returning to her seat at the table.

"Now *that* made my stomach clench up. The windows were being *forced open* a little at a time, by tendrils of fog that were reaching up from the ground outside," he shuddered at the memory. "I remember feeling an overwhelming sense of fear. Just a really fundamental, cave man kind of terror. Something was terribly, terribly wrong. Outside the windows, instead of the early afternoon sunshine I'd come in from, the landscape kept *shifting*. First it was just grass and trees, then suddenly I was seeing a desert, then just as abruptly as if someone had changed the channel, I saw waterfalls and then," he paused, shuddering. "Then a void. An emptiness. I think now it was outer space I was seeing, but I didn't know it at the time." He set the coffee cups he'd been extracting from the cabinet on a tray and paused, seeming to relive the moment. We all sat, silently transfixed, the only sound the burble and grind of the coffeemaker.

He turned to face us, his eyes distant, one hand absently fingering the embroidered flowers on the tea towel he'd slung over one shoulder. He grinned, ruefully. "I stood there, as my dear mother would say, 'useless as tits on a bull', my feet glued to the floor. I had no idea what to do, or what to think. Then, out of the blue, the ground began to shake." I noticed dad unconsciously gripping the counter he was leaning against, as if to steady himself.

"The desk where Maka was sitting rocked hard, then slid backwards and hit the wall. Clara Mills' ghost swayed and she looked around. I could see shock and fear registering clearly on her insubstantial face. Then Maka made this graceful leap from the desk to her feet, and landed, instantly steady. She took in the whole situation with one quick glance. She began chanting." His voice glowed with the respectful awe that he'd felt in that moment, watching Maka work.

"It was a spell, of course," he said, glancing knowingly at Lorraine. "But again, that was one of so many things I didn't know at the time. My impression was of a wild, musical invocation that sent the tendrils of fog spinning into a vortex in the center of the room. The rest of the room was in chaos. Books flew off shelves, a piano slid from one end of the room to the other. The fog was forcing the windows open wider and wider.

"I felt my paralysis fall away, watching Maka's quick actions, and my feet ran me right into the room, my better judgement a step or two behind." He grinned, and winked at my mom. She smiled back, pride and exasperation equally visible on her face, and shook her head at him.

"I dodged around the furniture, managing to only bruise and miraculously not break any bones in the process, and made it to the windows. At that point, apparently feeling like I was ten feet tall and bulletproof," he rolled his eyes ruefully, "I reached out to close the first one, just reached right into that fog not even thinking." He winced at the memory.

"What was it?" Jen demanded.

"The fog was so cold it damaged his hands," my mom took over the story. Her objective, healer-voice lightly tinged with her more emotional, mom tone. "I treated the wounds later. Whatever the temperature of that stuff was, it was cold enough to nearly freeze his flesh at just a touch, which is crazy talk, according to Earth physics. He's lucky he didn't lose them both."

"How did you do it, then?" David demanded.

"I pulled my denim jacket up over my back and grabbed it in both hands. That covered my hands and arms, and I was able to slam down the windows and get them locked. And I did it really really fast. And while I did that, Maka continued to chant and Clara Mills' ghost was pushing at the fog that had gotten inside, somehow, without touching it at all. She was corralling it for Maka so that Maka's spell could destroy it.

"It was probably the sum total of two minutes between the time that I paused outside the office door and the moment when that last tendril of fog was zapped out of existence, but it felt like an hour to me. When it was over, I just stood there, stupidly, staring at these two unbelievable women with me in the half-destroyed room, wondering what to think. I was teetering around on this precipice; leaning one way would take me down the path of denying any of this had ever happened, and spending my whole life trying desperately to make myself believe that. Leaning the other way meant looking at the world at an entirely new angle, which to be honest, held just as much trepidation as fascination for me. I suspect that trepidation had a lot to do with the burning pain in my hands at that moment."

"What decided you?" I asked, fascinated at this dive into my dad's mind.

"Maka walked over and took my hand and looked at the palm." He held it out for us to see. I'd known he had a scar there, but it was old and I'd never paid all that much attention to it. Now that I looked, I realized what I was seeing. The icy fog had burned a shape into it, the shape of a triangle inside a circle.

"*The Mark*, Maka told me. *The Mark of the Guardian. One who would be aided by the Power of the Triad.* Which made absolutely zero sense to me, but somehow, as she said it, an overwhelming feeling of *rightness* came over me. Like, I was remembering something that I already knew. Knowledge of things I was as familiar with as the back of my hand came flashing at me out of a memory I was, up until that moment, blissfully unconscious of. Bits of stories, of worlds, of languages and gods and peoples flowed over me, but most importantly there was this assured sense that I knew that I would become the Guardian, because I already was the Guardian."

And so, it began.

You see, Clara Mills had not died of natural causes. On that spring day in 1940, she'd been practicing a composition she'd been writing, on her office piano, which turned out to be the worst possible place for the task. That room, that particular locus in the universe, was a Portal. With the proper magics, the Portal could be opened and a pathway to Paradise, that dark place at the center of the multiverse could be gained. Clara didn't know squat about magic or intergalactic space travel or any of the rest of it, but she did know about music, and as it turns out, music can be a key. The music she'd been playing on her office piano that day had triggered the opening of the Portal. While Clara was marveling at the miraculous event her melody had inadvertently triggered, unbeknownst to her, alarms created by the Pilgrims were sounding all across various galaxies. Alarms from both magical and scientific listening devices that were attuned to exactly the sort of cosmic phenomenon that was currently unfolding in the office of the C.C. White Music Building on a little campus in the north part of the not-terribly-exciting city of Lincoln, Nebraska on the twelfth of April, 1940.

A figure appeared, tall, hooded, and inhuman, in Clara's office. Terrified, she sensed that no matter what else she did, she needed to protect this place, this Portal, from the creature who had materialized there with ill intent. Clara was no warrior, and her life ended that day with little difficulty on the part of the mysterious creature who had responded to the alarm. But what Clara was, down to her core, was a musician. The music she'd composed had opened the Portal, and she understood instinctively that her music was the key. Down to the final seconds of her life, with the creature's steel-cold grip around her neck, gasping for air, she played her piano, and the Portal closed. She used the same notes, the same melody that she had used to unlock the door to secure it again. She lost her life protecting it, but she did it. She closed the doorway, and as she lay dying, she bore witness to the hooded figure leaving this reality and returning to its own, in empty handed defeat.

"Since then," dad went on, setting the tray of full cups on the table and resuming his seat, "Maka has been working with us to keep the Portal safe and invisible. We've layered the place with, thanks to Maka and your Mom's tireless research," he smiled respectfully at mom. "Amazingly subtle and complex protective magic. "

"What happened when they tore that old building down, what year was that, sometime in the early 70's?" asked Rakow, waving off Lorraine's offer of creamer.

"Oh, yeah. That was a mess," Dad agreed, nodding. "We were there every day, or more specifically every night, layering the ground with spells and providing a new safe harbor for Clara in the Old Main building, next door, where she could watch over the space. Seemed like I spent more time driving back and forth to campus that year than doing anything else."

As I recall, that conversation devolved quickly at that point once Rakow and Dad started talking about the *Seafoam green 1953 Ford with the whitewall tires* he'd been driving that year. The one with the flathead V-8 that would go up to *at least* 50 mph in second gear. *It was a honey!*

Now, at last, the team was all on the field, David liked to say. We'd spent the last couple of years learning with Dad and Maka and the others how best to protect the place. We didn't know how long the Portal would continue to exist in that space, that was one of the trickier bits about finding Paradise. The portals moved around. But while this one stayed here, and open and accessible in our little corner of the world, we would do whatever it took to protect it from the Pilgrims. And taking our lesson from Malinowski, we'd probably continue protecting it forever.

To that end, we'd studied. A lot. Or at least I had, and then passed the *Cliff's Notes* versions along to Jen and David. We poured over stories describing the tactics the Pilgrims had used, written by the very few survivors. We quizzed Malinowski until he was loath to see us coming. We worked out physical strategies with Mr. Rakow, magical strategies with Maka and Lorraine, and triage strategies with my mom. Maka, Malinowski, Barb and Alesta were in and out, chasing down reports of Pilgrim activity across the galaxy, and trying to make it back to town to check up on us whenever possible.

And when we weren't busy with all that, we finished up junior high and started high school. David and Jon even continued to run track, and David had convinced the football coach to let him at least work out with the team, although his glass eye still kept him from competing. Jen tried to keep her hand in with drama, and managed to be in at least one of the major school productions each year. I spent progressively less time at the public library as my own collection of arcane texts continued to grow, with the aid of Maka and my mom.

And so, I was pleasantly surprised and only slightly weirded out on a Friday afternoon near the end of our tenth-grade year to walk into the final class of my day and see, instead my regular English teacher, Mr. Strange (yes, that really was his name) my favorite librarian, Miss Jeanne!

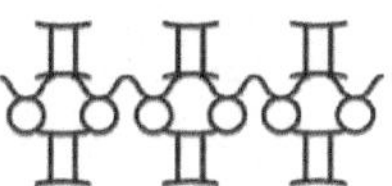

I GRINNED, GAVE a half wave and slid into my seat, squashing a momentary surge of social-anxiety ridden, worlds-colliding adrenaline. I'd always liked the fact that my library world was separate from my school world. The library served as my safe haven when school was angsty and rotten. And at the same time, I hadn't been there as much, lately. And I was already stressing about finding time to volunteer again this summer. Eek.

From his desk in the corner, Mr. Strange watched as we all variously thumped down backpacks and tapped pens in mild anticipation. Any break from discussing

Death of a Salesman was a welcome one, especially on a beautiful, spring afternoon.

Mr. Strange cleared his throat and we all settled down.

"Ms. Jeanne is here today from Bethany Branch Library to talk to you about some upcoming volunteer opportunities at the library this summer. Don't forget, volunteering is a valuable resource when it comes for applying for colleges and scholarships, so if you haven't already started doing it, now's a good time. Please give Ms. Jeanne your complete attention while I decide, based on these chapter quiz scores from yesterday, how much homework you're going to have over the weekend."

We all groaned and most of us turned toward Miss Jeanne as politely as a group of 15- and 16-year-olds are capable of.

"Before I start telling you about volunteering, let me tell you about this amazing book I just found that I bet some of you might like!" And she was off, pulling me into a story by some way-out sci-fi author called Orson Scott Card and his futuristic fight against mysterious aliens — and maybe I over-identified with the character, *Ender*, some. Or maybe a lot. My life was so not normal.

After class, Miss Jeanne quirked an eyebrow at me and mimed walking out together, so I hung around and waited while she packed up her things.

"Do you think you'll be volunteering this summer, Angie? It seems like after junior high, so many of my regular volunteers get so busy with extra jobs and projects, they just don't have time for the library," Jeanne mused as we walked down the third-floor hallway toward the exit.

I cringed a little, inwardly. I loved my usual hour or two each week shepherding the little neighborhood kids through the Summer Reading Program at the library. I'd done it without fail for the past four summers, but she was right. The demands on my time were increasing.

Unlike most kids, my projects involved a lot more magic study and demon hunting than summer school and job hunting. Jen, David, and I were far more likely to get moonstruck from late-night monster adventures than sunburned from high-noon pool parties. But spare time to do comfy, normal-kid things was indeed tight.

"Yeahhhh," I mused. "I think I'm going to have to check schedules with my folks before I sign on the dotted line this year. I'm sorry. How are you set for new kids this summer?" I tried to put a positive spin on it as we navigated the stairwell.

The building was emptying out quickly. Beautiful sunshiny Friday afternoons were not to be squandered. Not many kids were hanging around. We made it to the first floor and walked toward the main exit, nearest the office.

Whatever Miss Jeanne's reply to my question was, it got drowned out by the primal scream of jealousy that exploded inside my head when I saw that Jon, waiting for me at our usual spot, was not alone.

He was standing there with Michelle. Perfect Michelle with the perfect hair, perfect body, and perfect smile. She was leaning over his handlebars, pinning him in place while she laughed and executed a perfect hair flip. I was suddenly uber conscious of the fact that my own hair was crammed into a half assed pony tail. I reached up to touch it and discovered not one, but two pencils stuck up there. I yanked them out, cringing.

I think I might have growled or something, because Miss Jeanne turned and looked first at me, then at Michelle, who was dripping perfect laughter all over MY BOYFRIEND.

"Are you okay, Angie?" Miss Jeanne asked.

"Yes," I replied through clenched teeth. "This girl is tenacious. Jon is super nice about it, but she just won't lay off," I muttered, muscling open the heavy front door and trying to keep a civilized tongue in my head, as my mother would say.

Miss Jeanne smiled knowingly and followed me down the stairs. "What's her name? I'll see if I can occupy her attention while you two make a getaway."

I grinned at her conspiratorially. "It's Michelle. You're the best!" I whispered.

We swooped up to them and Miss Jeanne sang out brightly, "Hi Jon! Hi, Michelle isn't it? I haven't seen you at the library in quite a while!" She opened up the padfolio she used to carry her presentation supplies and carefully extracted three Summer Reading bookmarks. Glitter flew out with them and shimmered around us. "Sorry," she laughed. "Storytime crafts get everywhere. "Anyway, even if you guys are too busy to volunteer this summer, here are some great titles to have on hand for fun reading, and on the back are some classics that will for sure help you out on your SATs!" She tucked one each into Michelle's and Jon's backpacks and passed a third one into my outstretched hand.

I got a little rush from it. Must be my inner nerd rubbing her hands together, I thought.

"Say Michelle, don't you have a little sister at Mickle this year? I was just there last week." Jeanne turned strategically, giving me and Jon a clear escape route. I winked at him and we turned toward home.

"SO HEY, HONEY Bee, how was your day?"

He'd started calling me that when he'd discovered that my middle name started with a B. It had spawned a number of cute nicknames, including Angie Bee, Busy Bee, and of course Honey Bee, which was my hands down favorite. It never failed to give me a warm happy feeling in my middle. Today it felt like happy fireworks. I grinned at him, reveling in the sparkle in his eyes and the dimple on his cheek when he smiled back. I allowed myself to be distracted from thinking about Michelle.

"Pretty okay. It was cool to have Miss Jeanne instead of going over all the stuff everybody got wrong on the reading quiz."

"Ah yes, good old Willy Loman."

"Argh. I'll be so glad when we're done with it. I think our next book is either going to be by Toni Morrison or Zora Neale Hurston. How was your day? Did you get that math test back?"

"Yep!"

"Did you ace it, as usual?"

"Missed one, but I nailed the extra credit. 102% for this guy!" He pointed at himself with both thumbs and winked at me.

"Wicked!" I exclaimed. "What shall we do to celebrate our combined intellectual awesomeness?" I was hoping he'd say something like going to the mall or an evening walk to the park, someplace where we could sneak in a little making out. To be completely honest, at that particular moment in time I was more tempted than usual to not worry one little bit about who might be watching us and just start making out with him right there on the sidewalk in front of the whole world. He just looked so terribly handsome and kissable.

Down girl, I told myself.

I didn't often feel so intensely this way, but today Jon just looked so … *fine*. That was the word. Jon looked so fine, and judging by his adorably crooked smile, he was feeling the same way about me. My heart attempted a salsa beat, and found it pleasing.

"I do have one idea," Jon said smiling, "but I don't know what you'll think of it. There's a party tonight," he trailed off hopefully.

I cocked my eyebrow at him. Parties weren't our usual speed. We'd been to one or two, but they mostly involved semi- or mostly-drunk kids wandering around, doing and saying stupid stuff to the tune of music loud enough to eliminate conversation in somebody's basement or garage. The big excitement was usually just bailing out before the parents or the cops showed up. Exhilarating for sure, but not terribly satisfying. Plus, our folks weren't big on letting us go to them, so there was always an uncomfortable amount of subterfuge involved. Still, there could be making out.

"Oh yeah? Whose parents are out of the house this evening?"

"Well," he said, looking slightly uncomfortable. "Michelle's."

The warm fuzzy of my happy mood began to turn cold and prickly.

"Michelle Devlin?" I asked.

Jon flushed a little, then cocked his head and peered at me curiously. He rubbed at his temple. "Yeah. That's what we were talking about when you and the librarian came outside. She and Melissa and Heather are throwing it."

"Oh, yeah?" I asked, feeling tension building in my shoulders and acid rolling in my stomach. Jon seemed to notice, but he decided to soldier on anyway.

"Yeah, a bunch of us were talking about it in Social Studies." He paused to dig something out of his pocket. "Here, look."

He handed me a smudged photocopy of a band flyer, featuring a dark picture of two guys and two girls standing in front of a graffitied brick wall looking artistically nonchalant.

"This is the band I was telling you about, do you remember? The guitar player graduated last year and the rest of the band go to the University. They're supposed to be amazing!"

"And they're playing at Michelle's house party?" I asked doubtfully.

"Yeah!" he replied, excitement sparkling in his green eyes. "One of them is Michelle's cousin!" He stabbed a finger at one of the guys. He's the bass player. C'mon, Honey Bee, it'll be fun!" He took my hands and rubbed his thumbs over the backs of them. I noticed a little glitter from the library bookmarks had found its way onto my fingers. I grinned. His eyes were so beautiful and hypnotizing. I was on the verge of saying yes, despite my reservations when a car rumbled by and honked.

It was a big, old, maroon colored Ford, pausing in line behind a green Pontiac at the stop sign. I don't know who was driving, but hanging out the passenger side window was Michelle. Heather was in the back with Melissa and all three of them were waving and laughing and yelling out the open windows.

I tried as hard as I could not to let the jealousy I was feeling show on my face. Jon gave a friendly wave as they passed without taking his eyes off me. He smiled that adorably crooked smile and my heart melted anew.

"Ohh-kay," I said, only a little tiny bit begrudgingly.

"Stellar!" Jon did an excited little hop step and kissed

me soundly. This band must really be excellent. I'd rarely seen Jon this amped up about anything, laid back and chill was more his usual vibe. He took my hand and pulled me along, my dark mood improving slightly, buoyed by his good humor.

Just then, David and Jen caught up with us. They'd both been running, but neither was out of breath. Mr. Rakow was regularly on us with new training drills, which Jen and David took to like ducks to water. I was far more athletic by this point than I'd ever imagined I could be, but when I ran, I still got winded. My sour mood threatened to return.

"Did she say yes?" David asked Jon, and before he could answer turned to me, "Did you say yes?" His smile was big and hopeful.

I sighed. "I said yes."

The boys leapt and cantered ahead, swapping high fives and jockeying around like a couple of goofballs. Jen took my arm and matched her pace to mine.

"This party tonight has them both acting like fools," Jen said in a placid, observational tone.

"It would have to fricking be at Michelle's house," I grumbled.

Jen stopped, pulling my arm until we were facing each other. She studied me calmly. Carefully, with one long red nail she pushed my pouty lower lip back into its regular configuration.

"Jon loves you, and he knows trouble when he sees it." She paused, and cocked her head first at me, then at the boys cavorting along ahead of us. We'd turned the corner and were now walking down a quiet side street. The sidewalks were irregular here, so we usually just walked in the street. The after-school sounds of shouting kids and revving engines was fading into the distance. "I wonder." she trailed off.

"What is it?" I asked. "Please tell me an evil witch has put a spell on both of them, because I'm seriously not game for a whole summer of loud drunken parties at frickin' Michelle's house. I don't care if her cousin's band is the second coming of the Rolling Stones."

Jen frowned.

"What? Is something going on? Something work-related?" Jen's prophetic abilities had continued to grow and evolve over the last two years. It had strengthened her intuitions, or maybe leaked into them, who really knew? She paid extremely careful attention to it, and had become so observant that sometimes I worried it caused her to be overly vigilant. I tried to remind her, when it seemed to be getting too heavy, to rebalance her focus on the real, non-magical world.

"Are you sensing something? Or just hunting unicorns?" I asked.

"Not sure yet," she said. She looked at me and grinned. The moment passed. We resumed our pace.

"What excuse are you going to give your mom to go to the party?" I asked.

"Oh, I don't know. Probably a late movie at the mall."

"What's showing? Will your mom let you have the car?"

"I don't know. I'll ask about the car. Will you call the theater?"

"Sure," I said. "I'll call when I get home." This was decades before it was possible to pull your phone out of your pocket and ask Siri, *What movies are playing tonight?* We felt pretty advanced when the theaters first got recorded messaging so you didn't have to ask an actual human, you could just listen to them run through the movies and times without worrying if you were calling after hours or anything. Ah, technology.

Jon and David were standing at my driveway, waiting for us to catch up. Jenny and David took off across the street towards Jen's house, and Jon followed me into the carport for a little canoodling until Mallory got home and started her usual, "Cut that out or I'll tell Mom!" routine.

"I'll check the movie times and call you," I said, sneaking in one last kiss.

"Cool, and don't worry, you know you're the only Bee in my bonnet," he replied smiling. I hugged him tightly.

"You go. I'll call you guys in a few and see you later." I replied.

Jon grinned, but then grimaced.

"What's wrong?" I asked, concerned.

"Just a little twinge of a headache. No biggie. It's gone now. Talk to you in a few."

I kissed his forehead and he jogged off down the driveway towards home. I watched him go, and noted that once he crossed the street, his pace slowed and he continued rubbing at his temple. I felt a stirring of hope. Maybe a headache would kybosh the party plan. But probably not. *Oh well.* I went inside to call the theater.

I didn't notice Jen coming back out of the house down the block, staring intently at her twin as he approached home.

My mom wouldn't be thrilled about us being out until nearly midnight, but since it was all of us together, I knew she'd say yes. I figured getting my homework all done ahead of time might garner me some goodwill, so after I got off the phone with Jen, I settled down with my books.

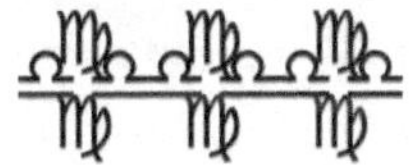

THE PARTY WAS a disaster.

Promptly at 8:30, Jen picked me up in their 1971 brown (technically *Mesa Sand)* Chevy Impala. It was a tank. It easily sat six, nine if you weren't particular about seatbelts or taking deep breaths. Jen had christened it "Clint" although I have no recollection of why.

The four of us had plenty of room to stretch out, and Jon and I took advantage of the space to snuggle and smooch in the back, while David rambled on at about 70 words per second about the band, their songs, other bands, other songs, lyrics, drummers who didn't live past the age of 33, movies, documentaries, Hitler's body-guards, and the Battle of Bull Run. Even for those of us most accustomed to his stream-of-consciousness ranting, tonight was exceptional. He was on a roll. I wondered if he and Jon had snuck a beer or two already. Jon was pretty meticulous about the oral hygiene when we were together, so he just smelled like mouthwash. I thought maybe more kissing might give me a clue, and then I pretty much forgot about David.

Jon and I kept one ear open each, and inserted "Wows" and "No ways" at appropriate intervals between kisses. Jen watched us all, and the road, closely. She parked us several blocks away from the party, as was her habit. Jen's stealth strategies were numerous and fre-quently useful. More than once we'd avoided the notice of neighbors or police by escaping monster-laden situa-tions by simply walking around a corner or down a couple of blocks before diving into Clint and making our escape.

We made a couple of stops, first the convenience

store for drinks and then we hit a drive-through for burg-
ers and fries which we ate sitting in the parking lot of
Bethany Park. Michelle's house was just north of Kahoa
elementary a piece. That whole area between 70th and 84th
streets is densely developed now, but back then, the east
half past Dorothy Drive, was still a hog farm. Her house
was one of those at the boundary, with neighborhood to
the west, trees and farmland to the east. A perfect place
for a loud party with a band.

They had a couple lawn chairs and card tables set up
in the garage, but the band itself was outside in the back-
yard. The hogs didn't seem to mind. Or at least, they
didn't complain to the local constabulary.

There was a keg, of course. Michelle had older broth-
ers and a single mom who worked a lot. A keg wasn't too
difficult to come by. Lots of kids brought bottles, too. I
was more of a puker than a drinker, so I had a big can of
Pepsi on board for my hydration needs. Jen had her iced
tea in a travel mug sporting some gas station logo. David
and Jon paid their two bucks each and were supplied with
red plastic cups and a sharpie. David's identifier was a
uniquely shaped starburst that always made me think of
Rocky and Bullwinkle cartoons for some reason. Jon's was a
stylized letter "j" with bee wings.

Swoon.

Jen was immediately engulfed by a small group of
theater friends, and David was snatched up by some jocks
and their adjacent cheerleaders. I waved hi to a few people as Jon led me nearer the band where he could scope
out the players and their equipment. He was, I knew, really hoping to be able to afford a new guitar soon.

His mom had managed a practice-quality electric for
him on his 15th birthday, and he played it until his fingers
bled and the strings would no longer hold a tune. This

birthday, he'd asked for cash to add to his new guitar fund. Lorraine had promised to let him apply for part-time summer jobs once school was out.

Jon and I found a space where we could perch against a brick planter and settled ourselves in to listen to the music. I got right away why he was excited about them. They played covers, of course, but they played them well and they had an interesting stylistic range. Joan Jett's, *I Love Rock 'n' Roll* was followed by *Twist and Shout* and the theme song to *Ghostbusters*. Both the bass player and the drummer were girls, and they were amazing. I found myself entertaining the notion of hooking up my oboe to an amplifier, just to see what it sounded like.

They played pretty steadily for the next hour or so. When they stopped for a breather, Jon stepped up to talk to the guitar player, and Jen hooked my arm and pulled me away to find a bathroom.

It felt stuffy and close inside after the cool, spring air outside. Michelle's mom smoked, and there were stinky, overflowing ashtrays on every surface. The smoke smell seemed to puff up at me from every step I took on the brown shag carpet. The house was about the same size as mine, but it felt small, as crowded as it was with bodies. The kitchen was full of kids laughing and drinking. We scooted past them and down the hallway where we joined the line for the bathroom.

The door swung open, two girls exited and two more entered wafting alternating layers of perfume, spilled beer and hairspray through the hallway atmosphere. I sneezed and imagined the hole in the Ozone layer above us widening perceptibly.

"The band is pretty amazing!" I said, and leaned against the doorframe of the bedroom across from the bath.

Jen started to reply, then paused and held up a finger. We were the only ones in the hallway at that moment. I could hear the raucous laughter coming from the kitchen, and the girls in the bathroom ahead of us talking. Jen tilted her head nearer the closed bedroom door and I focused that way as well, straining to hear the low voices, but it was tough with all the ambient noise around us.

Jen dug in her Levi's pocket and produced two super ugly earrings. I quickly took my left earring out and replaced it with the one she handed me. I'd scored these beauties at a family Christmas white elephant game. Tiny little Troll dolls, dressed like Santa. We'd enchanted them with an *Asculta tare* spell, which made it much easier to hear through the closed bedroom door.

"No way!" I recognized Michelle's voice.

"Yeah! She totally hooked me up after school! She said, *They're harmless, but it'll make him totally into you.*" It was one of the Michelle-ettes, but I couldn't tell which one.

"She's probably yanking your chain, girl." Michelle again. "How much did you pay her?"

"Just twenty bucks," said a third voice, this one giggly, probably tipsy.

"For one dose?"

"No, it's two. She said put one in his beer, and if you're not making out in thirty minutes, give him the second one, but if you do that, all bets are off!" She cackled.

"Hmmph," said Michelle. "I think it's garbage, but whatever."

"C'mon, Michelle, what have you got to lose?" Giggly voice again.

The bathroom door banged open. I jumped. Jen didn't. Sounds of movement from inside the bedroom made us scoot quickly into the bathroom and pull the door almost shut. Jen kept her eye to the crack and saw three girls file out of the bedroom. She closed the door all the way and leaned her back on it.

"Michelle, Jill, and Amy."

"Which Amy? Amy B., Amy K. or Amy J.?" I asked.

"Amy P. The one with the headband and pearls motif."

"Oh yeah. She's a Michelle-ette now?" I asked. We traded places.

"Since Jason asked her to Prom, I guess," Jen confirmed.

"What do you suppose they got ahold of?" I asked.

"Not sure," Jen said finishing up. "Could be uppers, could be downers." The two of us zoomed out of the bathroom in record time. We pushed past the three new pairs of girls now clogging the hallway, waiting for the bathroom.

"Or it could be magic," I supplied quietly, confident I wouldn't be overheard given the "CHUG! CHUG! CHUG!" resounding from the kitchen crowd.

"Could be they're after somebody else," Jen cautioned, threading her way between a group of three boys on one side and about six giggling, shouting girls who were in the process of trying to all fit on the couch together at the same time, and failing.

"Yeah, and monkeys could fly outta my butt," I responded tartly as we shot out the back door. We rushed over to where Jon and I had been standing to find that another couple was in the spot. I looked around frantically. "Where are they??"

"You go that way, I'll go this way," Jen said, pointing. She took off across the yard and I circled the house. There were kids everywhere. In little groups, dark corners, milling around the patio, filing in and out of the back gate, I kept my eyes peeled for Jon.

I was beginning to think he had maybe gone back inside the house. My thoughts were racing; *Was he okay? Was he with her? Where was she? What kind of drug or spell had they gotten their hands on? She could have anybody! Why wouldn't she lay off Jon?* Anger bubbled up inside me. I felt angrier than I ever had. Scary angry. I wanted to wrap my hands around her skinny perfect neck and—

—and I spotted him, behind the stage. Just in time, too. Michelle was sidling up to him, a plastic cup full of beer in each hand. I saw red.

I didn't pause, didn't think. I came up behind her and hit her low. I lowered my center of gravity slightly and strode directly into the backs of her knees to be precise. Not hard enough to injure her, but hard enough to make her fall and spill the beers. Which she did. All over Jon, who had gallantly reached out to catch her, sending them both tumbling into the band's stacked speakers, which collapsed towards the drum kit.

There was a screech of feedback, and cymbals crashing. People rushed in to extricate the drummer. Jen ran up and pulled me to one side, barely keeping me from stampeding over Michelle to get to Jon.

"You bitches! You fucking bitches! Get the hell out of my house!" Michelle screamed from the ground, staring daggers up at us. Her perfect hair was mussed, her perfect outfit drenched in beer. I failed to feel bad. Failed completely.

Jon had a dazed look in his eyes and was rubbing at his head. "What happened? Angie, what's wrong? Why are you—Angie, what did you do?"

"Are you okay?" I interrupted, blowing past his question. I frantically wiped spilled beer foam from his cheek with my shirt sleeve, wondering if it had to be ingested or if whatever it was would work through skin contact. I needed to get him out of there so I could check him out.

Jen helped me haul him to his feet and just then, some kind of wild whoop split the air.

Everybody froze. Even Michelle stopped swearing at us and raised up on one elbow to look. The kids helping the band right their instruments froze in their tracks to gape. Jen and I stopped trying to drag Jon away. We all stared, agog.

Standing in two lines along the back fence was about two thirds of the JV football team and quite a few of the senior varsity, too. Well, they weren't exactly standing, more like semi-crouched, knees bent. David was the only one standing, and he was marching up and down between the two lines, shouting.

"Kikiki! Kakaka!"

All the football players shouted in unison, "Ka mate Ka mate! Ka ora Ka ora! They stomped their feet and slapped their burly arms.

Jaws dropped all around us. David leapt around like a badass tribal warrior man.

Crap.

My anger morphed into acute embarrassment. I was familiar with the backstory on this. In fact, I may have been, ahem, sort of responsible for the fact that David was entirely familiar with this particular Maori tribal warrior chant. We'd been over at my place, working on our American History project, and my dad had the tv tuned to Public Television, which was not uncommon at our house. That evening, they happened to be broadcasting a Rugby match between New Zealand and Scotland. At the beginning of the match, the New Zealand team did what they always did, which was to perform a haka.

David was instantly glued to the tv screen. When it was over, he had a million questions for me and my dad.

It suddenly became critical to him that we find out everything we could about Maori culture and hakas. Because I'm me, I fed his interest. You're lucky, reading this now. All you have to do is jump on the internet and you'll have a half dozen YouTube videos to choose from. In 1987, it took more effort. But, because I'm a giant nerd, as we've established, it took more focused library research. I even found him some videos (thank you, interlibrary loan) and he watched them over and over again until he had it down. And judging from what was going on in front of us, he'd shared his passion with the rest of the football team.

A haka is a warrior dance. The words they were shouting were simple, "Tis death, Tis death, Tis life, Tis life, A step upward, Another step upward, The sun shines." What's really important is the vibe. It's ceremonial, for sure. It's done for special occasions, like before a Rugby match. But it's super badass. The dancers are warriors. Big, tough, muscle-bound warriors. They're looking to fire each other up and scare the bejeezus out of whoever they're about to pummel. There is eye rolling and knee slapping, stamping and bulgy muscle showing, yelling, and one bit where everybody sticks their tongues out, which is surprisingly freaky.

I suspected we were getting a sneak peek at a performance they'd been practicing for one of their upcoming games. I also suspected that it was being encouraged by excessive beer consumption.

The two lines of players continued their yelling and stamping, led by David. "A, upane! Ka upane! A upane, ka upane, whiti te ra!" A few of the players who weren't dancing were shouting encouragement. Other kids started hooting and hollering along.

Jen eyed me. "Maori tribal warrior chant?" she asked.

"Looks that way," I said.

"Where'd he learn that, do you suppose?" she asked pointedly.

"Um."

"He got the whole team to go along with it?"

"Seems that way."

"Seem hinky to you?" Jen asked.

That's when I spotted them. Amy and Jill, the Michelle-ettes, standing off to one side and holding a beer bong. For the uninitiated, a beer bong is a funnel attached to a tube. Somebody puts the tube in his mouth, while someone else pours a beer into the funnel. Poof. Instant stupidity.

Jill was holding it, and looking stunned. Amy was holding an empty cup, and smiling like the Cheshire Cat.

Crap crap crap. If they'd put whatever drug or potion or whatever they had through that beer bong, anybody who drank through it afterwards might have gotten dosed. But judging by his increasingly manic antics, I guessed their initial target had been David.

Jon groaned, holding his head. Jen handed me her keys and hissed, "Get Jon to the car. Drive it back here and get us, fast as you can!"

"But I don't have my—" I began.

Jen silenced me with a glare.

I zipped my lip and hauled Jon's arm over my shoulder and led him out to the street. We cut around the side yard rather than trying to maneuver through the house, and took off down the sidewalk. Jon was groggy and groaning, holding his head. I was completely freaked. I didn't know if Michelle had managed to get something into him before I got there, or if this was something entirely new, but either way, Jon was in bad shape.

The shouting and stamping and cheering behind us

was loud enough that porch lights up and down the block were flipping on and people were peeking out their doors and windows.

Crap.

By the time we got to Jen's car, Jon was walking a little more steadily, although he was still holding his head. I got the passenger door unlocked, ducked out from under his arm and tried to help him inside. He shook my hand off, and snapped, "I'm fine. I can drive if you can't do it."

His sounded pissed off, and in pain. I cringed. "No!" I exclaimed insistently. "You can't! You can hardly even keep your left eye open at all. I have to do this!" I ran around and got behind the wheel.

Jen and Jon had turned sixteen just before Christmas. David's sixteenth birthday was just a week or so off, but mine wasn't until September. I had my learner's permit, and I'd driven a little bit with my dad in the school parking lot after supper, but I wasn't scheduled to take driver's ed until this summer.

"I can do this. I can do this. I can do this," I muttered under my breath. Seatbelt buckled, key in the ignition. The engine roared to life. I started to check the mirrors and was momentarily blinded by a burst of fireworks coming from the direction of the party.

Crap.

I slammed the gear shifter into drive and hit the gas. The engine revved loudly, and the car stubbornly refused to move.

Crap!

Jon jammed his finger toward the pedals at my feet, "Emergency brake, Angie!"

Crap!

I fumbled to release the break and we lurched forward. Jon sucked in his breath and held his hand over his eye. I gripped the wheel tightly and drove the three blocks back to the party with more grit than grace. When we got close to the house, I lurched toward the curb, both feet on the brake and came to an clumsy stop.

Jen was leading David by the hand, still stomping and yelling, his tongue sticking out at a creepy angle. Jen motioned for me to open the passenger door. Clint the Impala was a 2-door. There was no time to fumble Jon and me both out of the front, find and trigger the seat release that folded the seat down, dive back into the car, and get David safely inside before the cop cars I could hear approaching were bound to arrive, and I really RE-ALLY did not want to explain any of this to my parents.

So, barely remembering to shove the gear shifter back into park, I unbuckled my seatbelt and dove over Jon, shoving him back toward the driver's side with my butt and pushing the passenger door open with my feet. Jen tried, she really tried to aim David into the car sort of gracefully. It just wasn't in the cards.

David tumbled headfirst across my lap and into Jon's, his feet still sticking out the door, still kicking and dancing. Jon tried to help, but he couldn't seem to get his limbs to move like he wanted. I tried to haul David in while Jenny ran around to the driver's side. The best I could do was to drag him a little further onto the seat and make sure I had a solid grip on his belt by the time Jen threw herself into the driver's seat and we sped off.

I clutched David around the waist to keep him from flying out. He was oblivious, laughing and singing, "Ki-kiki! Kakaka!" His feet were kicking and the open passenger door waved and bobbed.

"Get his feet inside!" Jen ordered.

I gave a huge shove, rolling him more onto Jon and catching his jeans enough to drag his legs the rest of the way inside.

"He's in!" I shouted, trying to make sure *I* was back in too before Jen cranked the wheel hard to the left and the passenger door slammed shut. I collapsed, breathless against the window.

David's joyously badass stomping and chanting continued unabated throughout. I struggled to get him sitting up. There was enough room in the front seat for all four of us, but it was snug and there really was no room for dancing. Behind us, red and blue lights flashing indicated the arrival of Lincoln's finest to bust up the party.

Crap.

Jen drove out of the neighborhood briskly, but not carelessly. Jon was slumped down holding his head and groaning. David was totally in his own world, stomping his feet, drumming his hands on the dashboard, happily oblivious.

"Where to?" Jen asked me.

"Can you find us someplace quiet where I can check these two out?" I asked.

Jen turned north and headed out of town. Back then, there were plenty of dirt roads and little cutouts leading into crop lands where a careful and creative kid could pull off and park for half an hour unnoticed. The Lancaster County Sherriff's department wasn't blind to such shenanigans, but there were only so many deputies to go around, and Jen's prophecy sense often guided her to the safer and most overlooked corners.

Before she could find a place, I climbed over David, pulled Jon into my arms and cradled his head. He was having a hard time keeping his eyes open, and any noise or movement made him flinch. I'd seen my dad suffer through a migraine or two, and this reminded me of that. So miserably in pain that the only relief is sleep in a silent, dark room.

He tried to push me away, and then cringed, as if it hurt to touch me. Jen and I gave him as much space as we could between us, and I reached for him with my mind, my blue crystal glowing brightly as I moved my healing sense into Jon's body to have a look around. I started in his head, and moved downward through his spine, and circled his heart. I took my time and checked him from stem to stern and I found nothing.

No injuries, no magic, nothing that I could con-cretely identify as the cause of the pain he was in. I felt torn between relief that it didn't seem like he'd ingested any of the potion Michelle and her Michelle-ettes had been playing around with, and about fourteen kinds of worry and anxiety about what was causing his pain that I was unable to identify.

Waves of concern and protectiveness poured through me, sending blue waves pulsing through Jon's body. I wanted so badly to protect him, to shield him from pain and keep him safe. Then adrenaline shot through me at the thought of Michelle and those girls. *I had to keep him safe from anyone who might hurt him, or try to take him away!* The blue waves pulsed in time with my heartbeat, speeding up and crashing as my heart pounded angrily.

I took a deep breath and tried to get myself under control. Mom had cautioned me many times to keep my intentions pure when I used my gift. Intentions were criti-cally important for a good result, she said. Bad or chaotic intentions could harm the person you were trying to heal. I loved him so very much! I stilled my angry thoughts and tried for a calm, protective, healing sleep and kept at it until I felt him relax back into the seat.

I blinked, and found myself looking at Jen who was

peering over Jon's slumped head at me. We were parked under a tree on the side of a gravel road. Peeking through the not yet fully leafed out limbs shone the bright light of a full moon.

"What is it?" she asked.

"Nothing!" I exclaimed, vexed. "At least nothing I can see. No damage, no magic. I can't figure it out!"

"Just a bad headache?"

"As far as I can tell, yeah. I tried to relax him to sleep, hopefully it'll let his own body take care of it. That's all I can do. Dammit!" I smacked my hand on the seat in frustration.

"What about David?" she asked, tilting her head at him. He was still actively juking around in the seat, grunting out nonsense syllables and beating on his biceps. He started poking at the radio controls. Jen swatted his hands away.

"He's not answering my questions, and his eyes are looking pretty weird. Can you do anything for our *Neville Bell* here? He's starting to freak me the hell out."

I grinned at her *Crocodile Dundee* reference, turned toward him and put my hands on David's head. He let me, but continued stomping and beating the dashboard, grunting and bouncing in the seat.

Unlike Jon, it was immediately clear that there was magic affecting David. *Damn those girls, playing around with stuff they had absolutely no idea about. Who the heck had sold this stuff to them anyway?* Whatever it was, they'd managed to get at least David, if not most of the guys on the JV team to drink some of it through that nasty beer bong. *Damn their eyes.*

A sparkly pink cloud was playing merry hell with his head. It was active, sending lightning-fast tendrils shooting out and zapping at his brain. Wherever it hit, explosions of electricity lit up that spot in his brain. It was horrifying to watch. The pink sparkles made it that just that much more so.

His frontal lobe was being zapped from all directions, and every time the evil bubble gum fairy storm zapped him, there was a resulting move or jerk or holler. There is a lot going on in our frontal lobes, like emotions, movement and creativity. Even more concerning than that was what was happening to his cerebellum. His 'little brain,' the part that controls thinking, language, and moods. That part of David's brain was lit up like a rave. Pink tendrils were all over it like a web, shooting sparks, which were met with vibrant green bursts, the color of David's necklace.

As I watched, I could see that the vibrance of those green bursts was beginning to fade. David's brain was being exhausted. That troubled me deeply.

David was a boundless font of energy. If he wasn't moving, he was talking. If he wasn't talking, he was thinking, or more likely, plotting. He was the spark, the game maker. The first to come and the last to leave. Whatever this spell was, it was causing all that energy, all that drive to expend itself all at once. And he wasn't in control of it. If I couldn't get this stuff out of his system, I was afraid it might drain him dry.

I reached out blindly towards Jen with my left hand. I felt her grasp it firmly and I felt her strength surging up my arm, into my shoulders, back, and brain. Infused with Jenny's power, together we hovered over the magical electrical storm that was cutting loose inside David's brain.

Storms. I knew something about storms. I ought to, having listened to all the dinnertime conversations between my folks about their storm spotting activities.

Storms grow when updrafts feed them from below. Once they get top heavy enough and full of enough energy, the lightning starts, and then the rain. The rain, in turn, increases the downward pressure, spreading out the disturbance, flattening it out. Squishing the life out of it.

What we needed here was a good, heavy downpour.

The thought had no more than coalesced in my mind when a purple cloud made of Jen's and my magic formed over the worst part of the storm.

Let 'er rip! I thought gleefully, and the downpour began. I won't say that the lyrics to Prince's *Purple Rain* didn't flicker through my consciousness just then, but my internal soundtrack in that moment wasn't brought to me by The Revolution.

It was the Fourth Act of Beethoven's 6th, *The Pastoral.* For the first three Acts of that piece, Beethoven gives us happiness and light. A summer garden party, perhaps watching the beautiful young couples arrive dressed in their summer best, peals of laughter, glasses of lemonade. A leisurely walk down to the water, a contemplative interlude by which to examine one's I'm-such-a-music-connoisseur navel. And then back to the party for another glorious romp with the Austrian nobility from the turn of the last century. It's the Fourth Act where shit goes off the rails.

From moment one there is uncertainty and fearfulness in the music. We can see the storm approaching. How bad is this going to be? He answers that question pretty post hasty; It's gonna be bad. He hits you with the big guns, the strings, the timpani, hard at you. You're in the storm. Drenched to the skin in a matter of seconds.

Jen and I were sure enough in it. We had waded in, hands held, preparing to pour much needed magical rain down on David's besieged brain. Fraught with one electrical strike after another, his emerald green defenses had slowed markedly. He was so tired!

Hang on, bud. Here comes the cavalry!

The cavalry rode in on droplets of purple rain which were promptly decimated by the electrically charged atmosphere. We ramped it up. Waves of blue and red energy flowed in from all directions, encircling and moving though the lightning strikes in a purple fog. The lightning continued to strike at us, but we were overwhelming.

We didn't just rain on this storm. We went fricking deep-tub-presoak-power-cycle-wash on this thing. We were ruthless. The lightning kept up until it simply couldn't any more. It faltered and shorted and cut out like the fluorescent bulbs in the girls' bathroom on third floor, until finally it was over, leaving Jen and me floating in a semi-luminescent purple sea.

We floated there for a moment, relieved and victorious. I felt Jen's laughter, and then in the very next second, I felt her fear. From our currently connected state, inside David, I understood it just as she did.

Fluid on the brain.

I didn't know how magical rain would appear on a CT scan, but I did know that fluid on a brain was not good, and magical fluid didn't seem to be an exception to that rule. We needed to drain the tub. But how?

I looked up. From where we floated, I could see the top of David's head, from the inside. That was the closest exit valve to where we were, but, yes! The top of his head – his hair! We have sweat glands all over our bodies, but the scalp is chock full of them. *Apocrine glands*, my anatomy study provided me with the proper term.

If we could raise the temp just enough to make some sweat happen, we could force this fluid up and out. I called to mind the last time we did the Presidential Fitness test in school. David and Jon looked up the stats for their age group ahead of time and decided to try to beat the high scores.

The one-mile run didn't kill me, but I wished it had. I'll never be the kind of person who runs for the fun of it, but David was. He and Jon would train at the school track day after day to try to beat the six-minute mile. Before long they were just doing it for fun and to one-up each other.

They'd come home, soaked with sweat, their hair plastered flat against their heads, sweat dripping down their temples. I conjured this gross image, and thought warm, sunshiny thoughts. Jen caught my drift and did the same.

The purple sea began to rise up, becoming a purple fog. In a hot minute, it was all evaporated. I squeezed Jenny's hand and we opened our eyes, peered at David to see if he was all right, and promptly burst into peals of laughter.

David sat back in the car seat, peacefully relaxed for the first time all night, eyes closed, a small smile playing across his lips. His normally dark brown hair shone a vibrant glowing shade of purple. He opened his eyes and looked at us in surprise.

"What? What??"

It took a while for us to calm down enough to explain the events of the last hour, and a little while longer to ascertain that the purple would in fact come out of David's hair with some scrubbing. With those important items accomplished, Jen fired up Clint the Impala and took us home.

Jon stayed asleep until we got back to my house, where he roused briefly at my kiss and gave me a puzzled look. Then he mumbled, "g'night" and his eyes closed again

I looked at Jen, the worry evident on my face. She said, "It's probably a migraine. They do run in the family. He'll be okay. I'll call you in the morning."

Still concerned, I nodded and clambered out of the back seat and quietly entered the sleeping house. I paused in my parents' bedroom doorway and was surprised to see Mom sitting up in bed.

Crap, what time was it anyway?

Mom pointed silently toward the kitchen. She stood and stepped into her slippers and snagged her robe from the end of the bed never once bothering to see if I'd obeyed the silent command.

Crap!

I slunk into the kitchen. The blue microwave clock said 1:27 am. I should have been home an hour ago. Then I caught a whiff of myself. I reeked of cigarettes and beer.

Crap.

"Where have you been?" she asked calmly, striding past me to turn on the little light above the sink.

"We went to a party. Some kids at school had a band." This was way beyond what a simple white lie might explain away. It was time for the radical honesty.

"Did you drink?" she asked, frankly.

"No." I replied, truthfully, grateful that I didn't have to add that particular nail to my coffin tonight, anyway.

"Who drove?"

"Jenny, and she didn't drink either," I said, before she could ask.

"But the boys did?" Mom asked.

I hung my head.

"I'll take that as a yes. Angie, I'm disappointed. The rules we have are for a reason, and that makes it even harder when you flout them. I expect more from you."

Anger bubbled up inside me again, for the umpteenth time that night. "Yeah, mom. I know you do. I'm terribly sorry I'm such a disappointment." I bit the words out, and they tasted as bad as they sounded.

A battle was waging inside me for control of my mouth. Her words stung! A big part of me, a really big part, wanted her to be proud of me. Like, I wanted her to think I was amazing and never screwed stuff up. And another really big part of me was yelling, *But wait, this isn't fair! I'm doing ten times more than any normal kid, or even than Mallory! And I'm still not living up to her expectations? For losing track of time?*

I threw my hands up in the air. "Fine. Mom. Fine. How long am I grounded for?"

She looked at me a little surprised. I very rarely did anything that landed me in trouble, and when I did, I was definitely not the backtalking kind. That was more Mallory's purview.

"Two weeks." Mom's voice was steady and neutral. She didn't like my attitude, but she was too smart to pick a fight with an overwrought teenager. She'd been down this path before.

"Fine." I said, deadpan. "If you're done with me, I'd like to go to bed."

"Yes. It's late. Goodnight." She turned on her heel and went back into their bedroom. She closed the door, quietly.

I blew out a big breath. I went into the bathroom, stripped out of my stinky clothes, tossed them down the laundry chute and held a warm washcloth to my face for a few minutes. It helped, some. By the time I found a clean t-shirt to pull on, brushed the worst of the tangles out of my hair and crawled in bed, I thought I might be able to sleep.

My brain had other ideas, though. After it treated me to the thousandth run-through of each time I had ever failed at anything at all in the last 15 years, I tossed the covers back and sat up dejectedly. I snagged a pair of jeans off the nearest pile of clothes I could reach and pulled them on in the dark.

If I couldn't sleep, maybe I could be useful. I'd go downstairs and read up on some texts in the den I shared with Mom that might shed some light on Jon's headaches. I snagged my slip-on moccasins. The floor in the basement was tile and it was way to early in the year for that to be pleasant on bare feet. I padded quietly past mom and dad's door, still closed, and slunk downstairs without turning on any lights until I was safely at the bottom with the door closed behind me. I shut my eyes against the brightness when I did flip on the overhead light in the main room. From there, I headed back towards the washer and dryer, deep in the bowels of the basement.

The cement floor all through the basement was tiled with some kind of stick-down squares, a checkered pattern of white and blue. It was worn, but pretty much indestructible, so mom and dad had never changed it. I snagged my gross party clothes off the floor under the laundry chute and tossed them into the washer with extra soap. If the smell was washed out before she woke up tomorrow, that'd be one less thing for her to be *disappointed* in me over. Ugh. I was in a mood.

The den was a room I didn't know our house even had. Mom had first invited me in two years ago after our world-hopping adventure that had revealed my dad's identity as the Guardian, and hers as a Master Healer. Once Maka had let my mom in on what I'd been able to do for Jen and previously for Jon, Mom decided it was high time to begin my training.

It was a room she'd created with her own magic, some illusions, and a little construction and wiring help from my dad. Mostly she created the space and he ran power and phone cords so they were available to her, but he may have helped with the magic too. They tended to work as a team, regardless of whose specialty the project at hand favored. Sometimes, I thought, they didn't even realize they were combining their efforts. It was simply the way they did business after more than 25 years together.

To enter the hidden room, you had to be leaning up against the washer and dryer, with just slightly more weight on your left hip. Then, by reaching up to the highest shelf, above the detergent and the bleach, to where mom kept the Woolite (for gentles) and the Ajax (for stains) you touched the funny old carved wood sign, upon which were etched the words,

Wash, Rinse, Dry, Fold, Repeat

A little push of will, a whispered, "*Nunc Placida*" and you tumbled forward into a dim, quiet room with bookshelves lining the walls, heavily laden with leather-bound tomes as well as newer, mostly medical texts. A huge, old worktable occupied nearly a third of the room, so tall it could be worked at standing, or perched on one of two intricately carved, three-legged stools.

When mom had first invited me inside, there was only one stool. Upon my second visit, the second stool had appeared, similar, but not identical to the first. The wood tone was a little lighter, and it was delicately inlaid with honeybees where the original was carved with ancient looking winged lions.

The stool wasn't the only thing that had changed in the two years since Mom had begun teaching me. A big, old, comfy chair along one wall had changed into a settee with a burgundy floral print. A nearby chest had become a large round table where you could set your teacup and as many books as you could possibly need at once, although a few invariably wound up on the floor. A nook with a wooden chair that sat in front of a tiny writing desk at the far end had grown into a room-sized alcove with more and more shelves, the writing desk had widened, and the chair had grown a blue velvet cushion with tassels.

A funny, crooked little pot-bellied stove sat in the corner nearest the worktable, adorned with a metal cauldron and flanked by shelf after shelf of spices, herbs, roots, stones, feathers and candles. That corner of the room always smelled good, and when mom would light candles while she worked, the whole den smelled like clean linens and outside and just a little bit like stew. It hummed with peaceful energy. This was a room of good ideas and good intentions, and it never failed to lift my spirit.

The den was lit from above by a combination of electrical power wired in by dad, and layers of spells laid on over years by Mom to bring the light to every corner, brightest above the worktable, dimmer above the love seat. I brushed the soft burgundy velvet of it as I entered the room and knelt to stroke the old Siamese cat's head.

Bast wasn't our cat. We didn't have a cat. In fact, we couldn't have any pets at all on account of stupid Mallory's stupid allergies. Bast was an elusive neighborhood fixture, owned by none, beloved *and fed, and spoiled* by all. We had no idea how she got in and out of the den – it didn't have any windows or access to the outside. Mom said if Bast could get in, then she was clearly meant to be here. She never bothered anything, didn't knock things to the floor like a naughty kitten, she was far too old and elegant for such shenanigans. She mostly slept on the love seat, or on a cushion by the stove when it was lit.

"Hey beautiful, don't mind me," I whispered into her sweet dusty ear, and giving her head a gentle stroke. "I'm just going to do a little reading before bed." She blinked at me once and returned to her nap.

I pulled several volumes on brain anatomy from the shelves, an article on inflammation and migraine, and a couple of spells promising pain relief and stacked them on the floor next to the settee where I could stretch out and read, provided I didn't get in Bast's way. I read and skimmed, I scribbled notes, I cross referenced spell ingredients with a chemistry book and a botanical florilegium. Nothing. I was getting nowhere.

I sat up and ran my hands through my hair in frustration. Nothing was just right. Maybe the problem was me. Maybe I wasn't sure what I was looking for. I hated not being able to figure out a magical problem just as much as I hated not being able to figure out a school problem. In fact, if I was being totally honest, I took pride in being good at academics, magical or otherwise. And I felt really stressed out when I failed.

Right that minute I felt like a total failure. I couldn't figure out what was causing Jon's headaches, or if there was any way I could help. I obviously couldn't figure out how to do anything right enough for my mom and nothing with Jon felt as right or easy as it had even a week ago, and I couldn't seem to figure out where we went wrong, or even what exactly was happening. I only knew that I was upset in just about all the ways you could be upset. Sadness, anger, jealousy, defensiveness and hurt were all vying for first place and it was overwhelming.

I stewed for a while in my angst until Bast, who had been carefully staying out of my way at the far end of the sofa as I fidgeted and fussed with my books, leaped gingerly down and stared up at me disdainfully. I looked back at her defiantly and asked, "What?" She turned her back and slinked deliberately and gracefully over to her cushion by the stove. She curled up with her back to me.

Great. Even Bast can't stand me.

I got up and drew Phyllida's book from its place on the shelf. Mom had increased my magical library a hundred-fold, but Phyllida's book was still my fallback for troublesome questions. I held it closed and thought as cogently as I could about John's headaches. *How could I relieve his pain? How could I discover its source and prevent it? How could I protect my love? Would the healing sleep be enough? Could I shield him?* My worry enveloped my questions, layering them with feelings of fierce protectiveness, anger at anyone or anything that might try to harm him and at myself for not knowing how to help.

I let the book fall open gently, my hands on either side of the warm brown leather, while Phyllida decided how she wanted to address my concern. To my surprise, the book didn't open to a page containing a spell, or notes on a topic she'd researched or any of the usual things she gave me. In fact, it opened to a blank page in the center of the book, which was nothing I'd ever seen before. I waited. Often Phyllida spoke to me in the margins, her writing appearing in brilliant purple ink.

Black ink began to emerge, but not words. A drawing? I watched in fascination as a field was outlined. Then came the colors. Greens, then pinks, purples and yellows, a vast field of wildflowers all entwined together and reaching up to the sky. Then Phyllida began filling in the sky with the colors of sunset, darkest in the foreground with a golden sun draped in purple and golden clouds, shining a final beam of sunlight across the field. Off in the distance, stars had begun to appear in the oncoming night sky, illuminating the darkness and reflecting celestial light back down upon the earth and lighting up a shimmering pattern of spiderwebs delicately constructed over the tops of some of the flowers. Busy, tiny creatures spinning silken threads connecting blossoms and leaves and stems glimmered in the starlight.

"It's beautiful, Phyllida," I said, my voice sounded frustrated, even petulant in the silence of the den. "But what does this have to do with helping cure Jon's headaches?"

On the opposite blank leaf, her usual purple handwriting appeared.

"Child, tell me. Which of these flowers is the most powerful?"

I frowned, puzzled. "Powerful?" I stared at the drawing. The flowers were each of them unique in color and pattern and position, but none of them stood out like it was more *powerful* than any other. "I don't know."

"What about the stars? Which is the wisest? Or the spiders? Which is in control?"

Again, I frowned. "I don't know, Phyllida." I tried to be patient. I knew she was trying to teach me something, but all I wanted to know was what to do about Jon and figuring out which flower was in charge of the spiders was failing to educate me. "Maybe the sun?" I took a stab at it. "Is the sun the most powerful?"

"Which sun?"

I stared at the drawing again and realized off to one side of the horizon, a second sun was beginning its rise. Wherever this was had more than one sun, just like the planet in *Star Wars* where Luke Skywalker grew up.

"I still don't understand. None of them? All of them?"

"*Perhaps you are beginning to understand, child. Each flower, each point of light, each reflective surface, each creature plays a powerful role in the whole. Sometimes a spider's web will ensnare a fly. The fly's blood will allow the spider to live another day. Other times, a spider's web will remain empty, allowing a fly to live another day. The flower cannot keep the spider from building her web, nor can the flower encourage the fly to either come nearer, or stay away. That is not the role of the flower. But without the flower, the spider would have nowhere to build her web. Without the sun and the rain, the flowers could not thrive. Without the gravitational balance of the suns, this planet could not maintain its orbit. Each of us must play our role, and each of us must allow the others to do the same.*"

Now *my* head hurt. Ugh.

Just then, Bast meowed loudly. I don't know if you've ever heard a Siamese cat meow, but *loud* is probably an inadequate adjective for it. I whipped around and looked at her, and noticed the light above the worktable flashing, indicating that the phone upstairs was ringing.

I looked at my watch. 3:16 a.m. Good gravy, how

long had I been down here? And who the heck was calling our house at this hour?

I glanced down at the book and saw one final line appear.

"*You must learn to listen, child. Not act, but listen. This is the way to learn.*"

I tucked Phyllida's grimoire back in its spot on the shelf and made to leave the den. Before I could complete the process, my mom appeared in her nightgown and robe. She looked like she'd just been told the sky was green.

"What is it mom?" I asked, picking up on her energy. "Is everything okay?"

"It's Donna," she replied. "David's mom."

"Oh no, what is it, is she—?"

David's mom had been in a nursing home since the accident with Mitch nearly four years ago. She'd never completely recovered her ability to walk without help, her memory was spotty on her best days, and her speech was confused. The doctors had tried all sorts of things, medicines, therapies, even a couple of surgeries but nothing made much difference. It was so very sad and difficult.

Since she had no immediate family, my folks, Mr. Rakow and Lorraine all did the best they could to keep her affairs in order, up to and including getting Lorraine named as David's temporary guardian. Jen and I regularly went to visit her with David, but it was hard. We never knew how we'd find her. Two weeks ago, she'd slept through our whole visit. We stayed about half an hour and then just snuck quietly out. Last week she'd been awake and confused.

"Who's there?" Donna rasped, struggling in her bed. The sheets were tangled and a glass of water sat precariously near the corner of her bedside table.

"Mom, it's me, David. I brought Jenny and Angie!" We came nearer so she could see us. Jen nudged the glass away from the edge.

"No no no!! It's dark, please, please help me!" she rasped in a faint whisper. Her eyes seemed not to see us at all.

Jen and I slunk out into the hall while David held her hand and listened to her half coherent whispers. Before long, she quit speaking at all and just cried unconsolably. David sat with her and stroked her back until she slapped him away and the nurse came to give her some meds. He exited silently and we piled in the car and took off, nobody knowing quite what to say.

David didn't like to talk about her. I never knew if it was because he couldn't sort out his feelings about her, or because he was just trying to avoid having any. We'd consulted my folks, and Lorraine about what we should do to help him, and they all said to just be with him, and be his friends. So, we went with him to visit his mom, and afterwards, sometimes we went out to Wilderness and ran on the trails, other times we went over to Mr. Rakow's house and played with Shadow.

"Is she okay? What's happened? She's not—" I stopped, mid-ramble.

"No, she hasn't passed away Angie. Just the opposite, in fact. She's awake, and alert, and she's walking on her own!" Mom's voice sounded hopeful, but her expression was puzzling.

"What in the world?" I asked.

"They don't know. The nursing home staff called just now. They said she'd gotten up out of bed and wandered all by herself to the nurses' station. They said she was demanding to know where she was and what was happening!"

"Oh my gosh," I exclaimed. "That's amazing! It's great!" I stared hard at her, taking in her furrowed brow and fingers drumming on the worktable. "Isn't it great?"

"Yes! I hope so, anyway," Mom replied, smiling reassuringly at me. She shoved her restlessly twitching hands into the pockets of her robe. "Your dad called Mr. Rakow and the two of them have gone to see her."

"Does David know yet?" I asked.

"No, your dad said he wanted to find out more before he called and woke everyone at Lorraine's."

"But, shouldn't we call? Doesn't he deserve to know?" Something about all of this was making me edgy. Or maybe I was still edgy about Phyllida's cryptic non-response about Jon. At that moment I felt extremely protective of my friends.

"I think," Mom said pensively, "I think we need to let your dad and Mr. Rakow find out more details first, and we'll all talk to David in the morning."

I stared at her. I couldn't figure out exactly what was up with her, but she was clearly hesitant which was unlike her usual confident demeanor.

"It's very late, Angie. You should get some sleep! Come to bed. As soon as your dad gets home, I'll wake you and we'll see what the situation turns out to be." She hustled me out of the den, through the laundry room and upstairs to my bedroom.

"Good night, sweetheart."

"Promise you'll wake me when Dad gets home?"

"I promise," she said, kissing my forehead and giving me a hug. "Now go to sleep. You'll be a zombie in the morning."

An uncomfortable image of Mitch crossed my mind, but I smiled and hugged her back. I shucked off my jeans and crawled under the covers in my t-shirt. I didn't think I'd sleep at all, but as soon as that thought crossed my mind, I was awakened to sunlight streaming through my bedroom window.

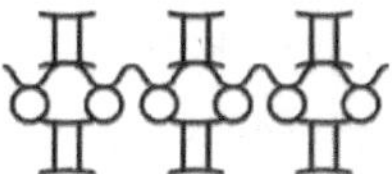

I SAT UP quickly in bed, trying to clear the fog from my head, knowing something was amiss and trying to remember exactly what. I scrubbed at my sleep-crusted eyes and yawned.

David's mom!

I threw off the blankets and pulled on the jeans I'd tossed to the floor the night before.

I heard a car door close and voices outside. I peeked out my window, the one closest to the driveway, and saw my dad leaning into the driver's side window of Mr. Rakow's car. Even with my window cracked open an inch I couldn't quite catch what they were saying. I grabbed a scrunchie off my vanity, crammed my hair up to avoid having to brush it, and stumbled into the kitchen.

Mom was sitting at the table, fully dressed, a mostly full cup of coffee in one hand. The newspaper lay open in front of her on the table. She was staring out the window at Dad and Mr. Rakow. When she noticed me, she carefully schooled her expression into a smile.

"What's the scoop, Mom? I thought you were going to wake me when Dad got home?"

"He did, about twenty minutes ago, but they've been outside talking. I tried to get them to come in and have coffee, but Rakow said he needed to get home and let Shadow out."

"Why talk outside for twenty whole minutes?" I asked, hunting in the fridge for the orange juice.

"I'm not sure," she replied.

"What are they talking about?" I asked, grabbing a glass and a cereal bowl out of the cupboard.

"I don't know," she said, and continued looking fixedly out the window.

I studied Mom. Again with the unusual. I'd never seen her staring at Dad with this wary expression, and I'd never known Dad to be secretive about anything. Well, unless you counted the whole, being the Guardian thing. But he wasn't secretive about that stuff with Mom.

"Well," I said, joining her at the kitchen table. "Here he comes. I guess we'll find out."

Dad stepped inside carrying a file folder with the nursing home's logo on it stuffed with a sheaf of paperwork. He set it on the desk in the living room before joining us in the kitchen.

"So, what happened?" I demanded while mom gave him a kiss on the cheek and handed him coffee in his favorite mug. It was a chunky, hand thrown one we'd gotten on a vacation to Colorado years ago.

"I'll give you some highlights, but then I think we should call Lorraine so she and David can be in on this right away."

My nerves settled. Dad's words sounded exactly like I expected, wise and fair and like he had a plan. I looked at mom and grinned hopefully. She nodded at me over the rim of her cup.

"The short version is, Donna awoke in the night with some regained faculties. She made it out to the nurse's station, very confused, and started asking questions."

"She's walking and asking questions, like, coherent questions?" I exclaimed. "That's fantastic!"

"It is, but I don't want either you or David to get your hopes sky high. We don't know if this is exactly a miraculous recovery."

"What do you mean?" Mom asked bluntly. Dad met her eyes squarely.

"I mean, she's walking, but it's still quite difficult for her. In fact, it appears to be causing her a good amount of discomfort, if not actual pain." Dad's brow furrowed and he frowned.

Mom and I frowned at each other.

"And she's talking," he continued, "but it's not exactly like she's back to normal. She recognized me and Rakow, which she's only been able to do on and off, as you both know, for some time. And she's asking a lot of questions, but we're not exactly sure how she's," his straightforward recitation faltered just for an instant, "processing the answers."

"What does that mean?" I asked.

Dad sighed and sipped his coffee. "At this point it means we have more questions than answers. Rakow and I were there for," he looked at his watch and stifled a yawn, "nearly five hours all told. The doctor at the facility checked her out, but couldn't tell us anything conclusive."

"How is she feeling?" Mom asked.

"Well now, there's the tricky part. After an hour or so of trying to communicate with her, she got pretty agitated. They finally resorted to sedating her."

Oh no," I said, dismayed.

"She has an appointment with the neurologist at 11:30 and a team of her doctors is converging at the hospital this afternoon to check her out and run a series of tests. Hopefully we'll know more later today. But for now, cautious optimism seems our best approach. We need to let the doctors look her over and see if they can tell us more about her condition and how to treat it."

We called Lorraine and decided to meet up at our house in half an hour. Dad took time for a quick shower and mom and I started throwing together scrambled eggs and cinnamon rolls.

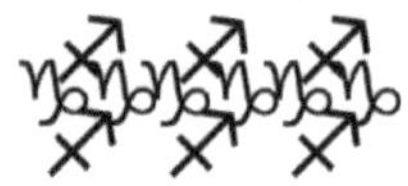

BY 9:30, DAVID, Jen, Lorraine and Jon sat around the table listening carefully to my dad's retelling of the events of the wee morning hours. Lorraine looked relatively alert; she'd evidently been the only one of us to get a restful night's sleep. I guessed grumpily that meant I was the only one of us who'd gotten grounded the night before. She set about carefully copying out all of the dates and times of the various doctor's appointments from the folder Dad had brought home.

Jen alternated between listening intently to Dad and carefully observing both Jon and my mom. Jon sat silently between Lorraine and David. He looked pale and wan, and had barely responded to my kiss hello. I couldn't decide if that stabbed-with-a-knife feeling in my heart was from his coldness or from my inability to fix what was hurting him.

David's legs vibrated under the table the entire time, completely unable to be stilled. His eyes were alight with a combination of hope and nervous dread.

"When can we go see her?" David asked Lorraine

once Dad had stopped speaking.

Dad held up one hand. "Son," he said. "You will, of course, get to see her as soon as possible. But I'm not sure that right away is best."

"Why not?" David demanded.

"Please dear," my mom interjected, setting down her coffee cup and meeting Dad's eyes pointedly. "If you have concerns about Donna's condition right now, I think David is deserving of your candor."

I stared at Mom, as did Lorraine. I really was not sure what was going on here, and it made me super uneasy. Dad cleared his throat and then addressed David directly.

"It's been a while since you lived with your mom, David. And I know that you've grown a lot since then, and that you understand some things better now." David nodded carefully at him, like he understood what Dad was talking about. "When I said that they needed to sedate her because she got agitated, I was being careful, because I didn't want to say anything that might bring up any old pain. There's a part of this story that Mr. Rakow specifically asked that I allow *him* to tell you about."

David frowned. His leg stopped jumping momentarily and he glanced at Lorraine, his eyes pleading. She pressed his hand and turned to my dad.

"Mr. Parsons," Lorraine said carefully. And then, when he didn't respond right away, "*Alden.*"

Ook. She used his first name. Something was definitely afoot. Tension thickened the air in the kitchen and it seemed hard to breathe.

"If there is something we need to know, now is a good time."

I'm not totally sure if Lorraine imbued that last bit with magic. I'm not sure she would have attempted anything like that on my dad, or any other magic user. I wasn't completely sure what the ethical ramifications of using magic to compel another practitioner to tell the truth might be, but it seemed both hinky and fraught.

The tension was broken by the sound of a car door slamming. We all turned to the window to see Mr. Rakow thumping up the driveway to the front door. His usually slight limp seemed more pronounced, the way it always did when he was tired. Or after a battle.

And his face! Oh my god.

"Mr. Rakow!" I jumped up from the table and ran to open the door. "What happened to you?"

A long, shallow gash ran the length of his right cheekbone. The whole area was swollen, and beginning to turn purple. His right eye was completely closed. By tomorrow, he'd have a heck of a shiner. Mom was standing at the kitchen doorway, ice-pack already in hand.

"Hey kid," he greeted me. "Thanks, Elizabeth." He accepted the ice pack, sat down at the open seat at the table and waved off Mom's gesture towards the coffee pot. Everyone stared at him in silence. He looked around at all of us, then at Dad, who nodded.

"You said you wanted to tell it yourself, Rakow. They're ready to hear. As ready as they can be, anyway," Dad said.

Mr. Rakow looked around the table at us all, then settled on David's face. David looked as upset as I'd ever seen him. His face was white as a sheet, his eyes were dark holes. He looked like a little kid who'd heard a roar from inside the closet in the middle of the night.

"Kid, your mom is real confused right now. She's been pretty out of it for a while now, and this," he gestured at his face, "I don't believe this was intentional."

David interrupted. "My mom did that to you." His

voice was full of pain and something else. An old-sounding understanding, laced with hopelessness. The fork he'd been using to poke at his scrambled eggs slid out of his fingers, forgotten. My heart broke into a thousand tiny pieces at the words.

Memories of David's life before Mitch and his mom were in the car accident, before the reality of monsters and magic had been thrust upon us, filled my head. I remembered the cigarette burns Mitch had made on David's legs and back. Even before that, the scrapes, and bruises, and welts. All sorts of little hurts that he would cover up or ignore. Things he wouldn't talk about, not even to Jen or me. Things that intensified when Mitch came around, but that had always been there, marking a long line of his Mom's boyfriends over the years.

At least I'd *thought* it was always the boyfriends.

Oh god.

Oh, David.

"Kid, whatever is going on with her right now, whether it's some kind of physical brain damage from the accident, or being so long sick with it, or even if it's something that happened back when Mitch got his damn fool self possessed by that demon, we just don't know. But right now, it's got her real messed up. When she wasn't shouting at us or crying, she was hurling stuff around and raising hell. I just happened to get in the way, that's all."

Mr. Rakow hadn't stopped looking right at David the whole time he was talking, and he had one hand on David's arm.

"Whatever this is, we need to give the doctors time to do their thing. Run their tests, look in their dang test tubes, whatever they do. Hopefully they can find something that will explain this, and they can fix her up. Maybe it's a medicine thing, or maybe a blood vessel has cut loose and is raising hell in her head. Aw, hell kid I don't know. I ain't no doctor. "But I know if you do go to see her right now, it's going to be real tough to see. And if you're going, you need to be ready for that, and your friends will need to have your back."

Mr. Rakow looked around at us. Lorraine had tears running down her cheeks. Jon looked shocked and pale. My mom and dad both looked profoundly sad. And Jen's necklace, and mine, were glowing fiercely.

David was looking down at his hands in his lap. On one side of him, Mr. Rakow still had his hand on David's shoulder. From David's other side, Jon reached out and took hold of his other shoulder. Lorraine put her arm around Jon, and then Jen on her other side. Jen reached out to me, then my mom and dad completed the circle.

For a little bit of time we sat, the circle of our hands and hearts and wills a living balm of healing magic making it just a little easier for David to breathe. Feeling his pain with him, sharing it, lessened it to a slightly more bearable level. I listened to my own heartbeat, slow and sad, but strong. I willed his to match my own. Tears spilled steadily down my cheeks, unrestrained.

Slowly, by degrees, the glow of the stone necklace under David's t-shirt brightened. Pale and flickering at first, it eventually it deepened to its strongest emerald shade. He looked up from his lap, and looked around at all of us. His expression was steady. It reminded me of the way he looked at Jen and me last year, right before we went inside that dead female troll's cave to see if there were any young left alive – like no matter what we found, it wasn't going to be good, but we were all going in together, and we knew what we had to do.

"Thanks," he said simply. Mr. Rakow gave him one

of those side hugs that guys excel at, and David scrubbed a sleeve across his face.

It was decided that Lorraine would take David, Jenny and me to the hospital to meet up with Donna as soon as the nursing home transported her for the first of her many appointments scheduled for that day. The others would follow as needed.

DAD WAS RIGGING me up with the handheld radio when the phone rang. He snagged it with one hand as he finished strapping the handheld to my belt loop with the other.

"Hello? Yes, speaking." His face tensed. "Was any-one hurt?" A pause, "She what?" He grabbed a pen and a pad of paper from the desk and scribbled notes in his largely undecipherable script.

I backed up into Mom, who had popped out of the kitchen, intuiting trouble.

"Where did it happen?" Another pause. "At what time? And cruisers are searching for her now? All right. Yes, someone will be at this number at all times. Please keep us posted. Thank you." Dad replaced the receiver absently, staring at his notes.

"What happened?" My mom asked, placing a hand on his shoulder. Everyone else had crowded around.

"The van carrying Donna from the nursing home was involved in an accident on the way to the hospital," he said. "No one was badly hurt, but the driver of the van lost consciousness for a few minutes. Once he was revived by the EMTs, he told the responding officer that his sole passenger reached up behind him, grabbed the lanyard with his ID around his neck while he was driving, and choked him unconscious. He ran a red light and was hit by another car. That driver is fine. She reported seeing a woman dressed in a nightgown and a bathrobe getting out of the van and leaving the scene on foot."

"What in the world?" Lorraine exclaimed.

"The driver of the other car," Dad continued, "said the woman got about half a block away when she was picked up by a blonde woman driving a green Pontiac 4-door. She didn't get a license plate number, but she was able to tell officers which direction they were headed.

"What do we do?" I asked.

"We have to start looking for her!" David exclaimed; his eyes wide.

"I agree," Dad said. That surprised me a little. I half expected him to urge caution and tell us to let the police do their jobs. He clearly had a different agenda in mind.

"The accident happened at 66th and Holdrege. Donna apparently walked north and was picked up by the driver who came from the north and headed east down a side street."

Mr. Rakow stepped forward, looking very *Sergeant Rakow* and started issuing orders.

"Lorraine, take Jenny and head north. Run the grid from Holdrege to "O" Street, 66th to 48th. David and I will take 66th east to 84th. Professor, you and Mrs. P. look west, 48th to 27th. Angie, you and Jon stay here and monitor phones and radios."

I nodded. Something was knocking at the edge of my awareness, like when there's a word on the tip of your tongue, but I couldn't quite grasp it. I handed him my handheld and Dad passed another to Jen. He and mom had one already in their car. Everyone quickly headed out to search.

Once the door closed on the flurry of activity, the silence of the house felt strange and heavy. I turned to look at Jon, perched on the arm of one of the living room recliners, within grabbing distance of the radio on the desk.

"How's your headache?" I asked, feeling oddly shy. He'd seemed so distant all morning, and granted, today was turning into a dumpster fire of epic proportions, but that didn't explain it completely.

"It's fine. I'm fine, Ang," he said dismissively. He wouldn't meet my eyes, focusing instead on some point in space off to my left.

Uh oh. *Fine.* Fine was code for everything was horrible and I'm ready to run away and live on a desert island. Gulp.

"Uh, ok, that sounds bad. What can I do to help?" I asked cautiously.

Jon glared at me. He actually glared. My insides went cold. Jon didn't glare. It just wasn't his thing. Holy cats, this was bad.

"That's just it, Angie. I think you've done plenty." Jon's voice was cold.

I'm sure my expression registered the utter shock I felt, if his giant eye roll was any indication.

"What—I, what did I do?" I spluttered. For the moment anyway, my utter bewilderment was overriding my anger, but I could feel that bubbling down in my gut, too.

"What is going on with you?" Jon demanded. "Was it totally necessary to lay Michelle out with a full body block? Seriously?" he asked, his tone confused and angry.

I froze for a second while a million emotions battled for first up to bat. Confusion, anger, defensiveness, embarrassment, nervous fear, exasperation and shock rounded out the short list.

"We thought she was trying to drug you!" I protested. "She DID drug David, and most of the football team! I was trying to protect you!"

"But she didn't, did she?" Jon countered.

"What?" I exploded. "What are you talking about?"

"*She* didn't do it. Jen told me what you guys overheard in the house. Jill and Amy tried to get her to use that stuff on me, and she wouldn't. Those two nimrods got David and the rest of the team with it, but Michelle refused to have anything do with it. She was innocent, Angie. And you *attacked* her." Jon crossed his arms and stared at me.

I stopped spluttering and stared back at him. "But we thought—"

"Yeah," he interrupted, exasperated. "I know that's what you thought. I also know you can't stand her and that you're jealous because she likes me."

"I—well, yeah!" I couldn't deny the truth of that. Confusion, anger and disbelief were all crashing down on me, making it hard to think straight, but he was totally right. Of course I was jealous! Uber mondo jealous of Michelle. But here he'd yanked my righteous justification for feeling that way – that she'd been trying to drug him – out from under me. Suddenly I was flailing. I knew I was still mad, but now I had to figure out exactly why, again.

"That's just it, Ang. It's not cool. Being jealous of her. It's not cool," he said, pleadingly.

"It what?" My brain was scrambling to keep up here.

"Look," Jon said. He sounded like he was trying to wrestle a bomb away from a monkey. "Michelle is okay. She and I have been friends for a long time, you know? Longer than you and I have been going together, for sure."

Okay, that piece of information was doing nothing to temper my jealousy. I was already fighting tears and the very strong temptation to say something stupid and hurtful.

"I could have dated her. I know she likes me, Ang. I've known that for a long time. But I never did. Do you know why that is?" Jon looked at me, his expression expectant, like he knew I wasn't a blithering moron and this was something I should be able to understand.

I felt like a blithering moron, but then again, I felt like he might be one too. We were two blithering morons trying to find our way off a cliff blindfolded. My insides were being crushed in a vice, my neck muscles so rigid you could have used them as bridge supports, and my footing was decidedly uncertain.

Some good angel encouraged me to squash down my desire to respond with, "Because she's a vacuous dipshit?" I forced myself with all the strength in my heart to listen to that angel, to try to put out this fire rather than fan its flames, and I responded instead simply with, "Why?"

"Because I love *you* Angie," he said.

My heart wanted to melt. It really did. But at the same time, he sounded confused. Like he just could not sort out why that was even a question and that aggravated me all over again.

Jon went on, "I've been in love with you for as long as I can remember, Angie. I guess I thought you knew that. Really knew it. But the jealousy thing, I don't know, Ang. It makes me feel like you don't trust me. Like you don't trust us." Jon looked down, his face sad and somehow younger. He was sixteen then, just blossoming into the man he might become, but this was a sadness that spoke of his eight- or ten-year old self. The face of the boy I'd known all my life, who'd been the more sensitive twin, the one Jen had both teased and protected. The one who looked to his mom for advice and counsel, who was easily hurt but always looking for balance.

I took a big breath and tried to look for balance too. Truth was, Michelle had not only done nothing wrong, but I supposed I should actually feel – ugh – grateful to her for turning down the temptation to go along with Jill and Amy's dumb plan.

Here I was trying to be the superhero and save the day, and I had aimed my ire at her, despite the fact that she was technically innocent. Okay, so she wasn't innocent of liking my boyfriend, but she had not acted on it with a $20 love potion from some fly-by-night wannabe witch, and that was an important distinction I had totally blown right past. My oh-so-carefully constructed bubble of self-righteousness shattered.

"Okay," I said quietly. "I think you have a point."

I flopped down on the sofa and covered my face with my hands.

Jon left his perch and came to sit next to me. He gently dislodged my hands from my face and poked my chin so I was looking up at him.

"Tell me this, Ang. Have I said or done anything that would make you think I like her more than you? Or that I want to break up with you or anything like that?" His voice was calm, but it was a heartfelt question. I could tell. I mean, he sounded a little defensive, and a lot hurt. But I knew Jon. I knew it was important to him what I thought and his questions weighed heavily on me.

I thought carefully about how this had all gone down. About how it made me feel when he talked about her or I saw them together. About how she was so perfect and pretty and how he was always laughing at stuff she said. I tried to put that into words that made sense.

"I think," I paused to wipe my nose on my sleeve. "I think it's not so much about what you're doing or saying, as about how she makes me feel," I said dejectedly.

Jon frowned at that, thoughtfully. He seemed to be connecting the dots in his head as I spoke. "What exactly do you mean? How does she make you feel?"

"Short!" I retorted angrily. "She makes me feel short and dumpy and too serious and nerdy and unlovable. She makes me feel totally inadequate. Like, how could you possibly like somebody little and nerdy and serious when you could so easily have someone tall and beautiful and bubbly who makes you laugh?"

That all came out sounding totally pathetic and I cringed, swiping at my leaking eyes. My stomach was in knots and I felt like a mean, little worm. The tears started flowing more freely and I stopped even trying to wipe them away.

He stared at me. I didn't know what to make of the stare other than he seemed to be processing what I'd said.

"That's how you *feel?*" he asked.

I tried to look away, but he gently turned my face back to his.

"Ang, look. A lot is going on here that I don't understand, but here's one thing. I don't think I can fix those feelings. I know for a fact that you're not unlovable, and I don't want you to ever feel like that, but I don't think it's my call. And to be totally fair, the other thing that isn't my call is who you can be friends with, any more than you can say who I can be friends with. I mean, like, what if I was jealous about how much time you spend with David? What if I'd kicked up a fuss about that whole week you spent camping without me, and with him *and* Malinowski?"

My eyebrows shot up at that, but then I thought about it for a minute. In all honesty, it was something I'd considered and dismissed more than once. I'd told myself my friendship with David was just, different. We had our thing. It was him and Jen and me and I felt like if anybody could understand that, it was Jon. But at the same time, if the Triad had been Jen and Jon and some other girl, I'd have certainly felt left out and probably stupidly jealous. Jon deserved every bit of credit for being awesome about that dynamic.

The idea of being jealous of Malinowski was laughable, he was not only too old, and attached to Barb at the hip, but he was totally not my type. That said, he wasn't completely ugly or uncool. I could see how things like our occasional training trips at Wilderness with him, even when Jen and David and of course, Barb were along could be emotionally tricky territory.

Jon deserved better from me than to simply dismiss this stuff like it was just expected that he would be cool with it when I couldn't even say the same thing about myself. But that wasn't all of it, and I thought maybe I'd put my finger on what was bugging me the most.

I sighed. "Look. I think you're right about a lot of things, but there's still this. It makes me angry and sad that you see how upset I get when you hang out with her, and yet you're more concerned with Michelle being treated fairly than how I feel. I mean, yes. It's true that I've have not given Michelle a fair chance. I'll admit that. And that's unfair to you as well, because you *have* given David and Malinowski fair shakes."

Here I took both his hands in mine, and focused strongly on making my feelings jibe with my intentions.

"But am I not worth being your main concern? If I am, like you always say, the only Bee in your bonnet, then shouldn't I rate your love and understanding over your anger that I'm not treating Michelle fairly?" I willed him to understand.

Jon opened his mouth to speak, and suddenly clutched at his head. His face went ghostly white from one second so the next. He groaned, a weird, breathless sound.

"Oh god!" I cried. "Jon, what is it?"

"I don't know," he gasped. "It hurts!"a

Sweat popped up on his forehead. I looked closer, then I stared. Then I panicked. His sweat was blue. *My blue*! Holy crap! Whatever I'd done last night to try to shield him, to protect him, now he was sweating it out and oh my god he wasn't breathing! His eyes rolled back; his face was deathly pale wherever the blue sweat hadn't trickled down. And his lips were turning blue, not my blue but lack of oxygen blue. Whatever I had done was killing him!

I grasped at his face, and I drew out – like I was drinking through a straw. I drew my magic out of him and then I breathed into him, with pure, clean ordinary air. Again and again, I drew the blue shield of magic I'd surrounded him with the night before out and blew in air. Like some weird magical CPR.

"C'mon Jon, c'mon, please I'm so sorry! Breathe Jon, breathe!!" In and out, tears pouring down my cheeks I breathed. "Please breathe please breathe please breathe."

I wasn't sure if I was chanting aloud, or if it was all in my head. My heart was racing in my ears. Time seemed to be speeding by, with every second that he wasn't breathing on his own a second closer to disaster.

And then, just when I was about to despair, he coughed. He coughed! And sucked air in!

Relief washed over me in a tidal wave. I stared at

him, shaking. Afraid to move, my own breath coming in gasps. I was so freaked out and shaking so hard, that when he started pointing and waving at something behind me, my brain refused to compute. My face must have mirrored my confusion because he finally coughed out, "Radio!"

Crap! The teams out looking for David's mom! The sound of chatter on the radio finally made it through my addled brain.

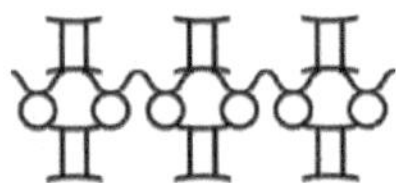

"…COME AS SOON as possible. Repeat. This is NØWCH calling NØZCA, NØBDE, NØZCD, NØVET, NØGRD, NØHLR. We've found her! Need backup. Please come as soon as possible." NØWCH was Lorraine's Ham Radio call.

"Roger NØWCH, this is NØGRD. What is your location"? My dad replied.

"NØGRD, this is NØZCJ. East Park Mall. North side, outside the record store. We have…visitors. Need backup ASAP!" It sounded like Jen had grabbed the handheld from Lorraine. In the background, indistinctly, I could hear a loud, demanding voice, and a quieter one, soothing.

"NØZCJ, this is NØZCD. Is she okay?" David's voice was tense. "Is my mom okay?"

Using the handhelds to communicate about some things was tricky in the sense that it was far from private. Anyone with a Ham Radio could listen in on your conversation, in fact could join in, provided they were appropriately licensed operators and identified themselves correctly.

Dad had insisted, nonetheless, that we needed them to stay connected, and had made us all study to take the licensing exam, which at that time included learning Morse Code. Sigh.

-... .. --. / ..-. ..- -.

"NØZCD, this is NØZCJ." Jen replied. "She's safe. Things are hinky. Get here now. NØZCJ out."

"On our way, NØZCJ. NØZCD out."

Hinky was code for our kind of trouble. Supernatural wackiness. Not the kind of thing she would detail on the radio.

Crap.

I looked at Jon. He was still looking pained, but he was breathing normally, thank heavens, and sitting up, rubbing at his temple.

"How do you feel? What do you think? Should we try to go?" I asked, nervously shifting from one foot to the other.

"I'm okay now. I don't know what happened, it felt like I was drowning!"

I cringed. "I think I maybe have an idea, but I'll explain later if you're really okay?"

"Yeah, my head still hurts, but not as much, and at least I can breathe. Ask your dad if we should go or stay? We have the bikes, we could be there in maybe 15 minutes, sooner if we book it."

I grabbed up the microphone. "NØGRD, this is NØZCA. Should we head over or stay here?"

"NØZCA, this is NØGRD. Stay put for now. Will advise."

"Roger NØGRD. NØZCA standing by." Energy

flooded my limbs, but had nowhere to go. I tried a couple of toe touches and stretched my hammies like I was getting ready for a run.

Just then, the scanner in my folks' bedroom crackled. Before he left, he'd tuned it to the Police Department's channel. The dispatcher's voice was its usual half-understandable garble of codes and officers' car and personal ID numbers that made little sense without a cheat sheet, but I heard a 10-15 code for a disturbance and the location was East Park Plaza. I scurried over to the bedroom door, midway between the scanner on my one side and the Ham on my other, trying to listen to both simultaneously.

An officer's voice reported a 10-23 that meant he'd arrived at the scene. The dispatcher came back with "Reported 10-91V inside the mall. Animal Control en route. Possible injuries. Proceed with caution."

"Roger, dispatch."

"1831, be advised. Store owner reports—" she paused and then continued, enunciating carefully. "Store owner reports, giant spiders."

"Please repeat, dispatch. I thought you said giant spiders?"

"Roger, 1831. Store owner inside the mall reports sighting – giant spiders. The size of Cocker Spaniels, she says. At least a dozen. She and ten or more customers are barricaded in their stock room." The dispatcher sounded like she was very carefully repeating exactly what she'd been told, as weird as it was.

Gulp

"Reports of injuries?"

"Two for sure. Fire and ambulance have been dispatched."

The channel started getting really crowded then with

fire and ambulance chatter overlaying the police talk. Jon and I stared at one another, wide eyed. Jen's voice came again from the Ham Radio in the living room.

"NØZCD, this is NØZCJ. I have your mom safe in the car. She's asking for you. ETA?" Jen's voice sounded calm, but in the background, we could hear Donna's voice, confused and loud.

"Where is David, girl? What have you done with my son? What is going on? Don't touch me!" Donna's voice was cantankerous, unlike the soft, breathy tones I was familiar with. "Where is he? What have you crazy people done with my son? Is he in a gang? What are you up to? Lorraine! Lorraine! What kind of craziness – good lord what are those??" There was the sound of scuffling, and a car door opening and slamming shut again.

"Let me out of here, girl! What have you done with my son?" Then there was a sudden radical shift in her tone, from violently outraged to plaintive and tearful. "David?"

Two things then happened at once. From the bedroom, on the police scanner we heard a familiar voice saying, "Be advised, 1826 is 10-23 at East Park Plaza."

"Roger 1826"

It was Officer Yardley! Oh, thank goodness! Officer Yardley was our friend on the Police force. He, like we, could see things other people couldn't. And if regular people on the scene were reporting Cocker Spaniel sized spiders, the heavens only knew what was actually going down. People tended to minimize what they saw that didn't make sense. The 9-foot-tall horned troll under the bridge we'd fought had first been reported as a tall homeless guy wearing a funny hat. The zombie takeover of the 7-11 on Garfield Street last year was reported as a gang incursion. And the hell dimension that opened up in the house off Piedmont was simply a natural gas explosion.

This was bad. Officer Yardley knew all about bad.

At the same moment, the Ham Radio in the living room squawked. "This is NØVET. NØZCA, we're here. David's in the car with Jen and Donna. Lorraine is holding the perimeter and trying to allow safe passage out for the civilians. Yardley is getting people out the fire door. I'm going in, NØVET out."

I turned to Jon, my wheels spinning madly. "Whatever this is, it's connected to David's mom, and it has bad magic written all over it."

"Agreed, Ang. But what or who is behind this? And what's their game?"

"We need to try to talk to Donna. Try to figure out what's happened to her, what made her wake up. Maybe she saw something, or somebody."

Jon went pale again and grabbed at his head. He staggered. I dropped the radio mic and grabbed him to keep him from falling. We lurched over to the side of my parents' bed and he managed to sit down, mostly upright, leaning against the headboard.

"Jon!"

"It's okay. I'm okay. Ang, listen, it's your dad."

I rushed back to where I'd dropped the radio mic, snatched it up and listened.

"NØZCA, do you copy?"

"This is NØZCA, please come again, dad."

"This is NØGRD. NØZCJ, do you also copy?"

Jen's voice replied, "NØZCJ, copy."

"NØZCJ, you and David get Donna back home. We'll make sure the situation here is contained and then meet you there."

"Are you sure you have it handled, NØGRD?" I asked.

"Roger, NØZCA. Stay put. NØZCJ, you and David get Donna out of here. Keep her safe and quiet if possible."

"Roger NØGRD," responded Jen.

"And kids," Dad said. "Whatever Donna asks, do not be overly forthcoming. Is that understood?"

Jon and I exchanged suspicious looks, but Jen replied promptly and pointedly. I got the feeling that whatever she was trying to convey, it was aimed at both us and at David in the car. "Ixnay on the hinky talk. Roger, NØGRD. NØZCJ out."

I helped Jon up off the bed and back to the living room sofa. Then I went and stood by the front door and waited the very few minutes it took for Jen to turn Clint the Impala into the driveway at an almost-safe speed.

David and his mom rode in the front seat with Jen, who looked stern. David looked like tightly wound wire. Donna looked fragile like a bomb. I dashed outside to help them get her in.

"You!" she shouted at me the minute I got to the car, her voice creaky and broken but loud. "I should have known!" I flinched. Then in an instant her voice changed from venomous to petulant. "You girls are nothing but trouble to my sweet boy!"

I stopped, stunned. Donna had never, ever acted like this around me. She'd been a little strange, often a mess, but she'd always liked me, I'd thought. Angel – it was her special nickname for me.

This was most definitely *not* the Donna I knew.

"C'mon mom. Let's get you inside," David said through clenched teeth. I helped Jen and David maneuver Donna up to the house. When Jen spotted Jon sprawled on the couch, she detoured to him while David and I got Donna settled down at the kitchen table.

She looked terrible. Her slippers were filthy and barely hanging on. The hem of her nightgown was splashed with mud and the sleeve of her robe was torn. Her hands were dirty and her nails were long and jagged. Her hair, long and brown, was usually kept by the nursing home staff in two long braids. They were a mess now, one was completely undone, the other was snagged with sticks and leaves, like she'd stumbled through a hedge or something. Her hands were shaking, heck, she was shaking all over.

"Let me get you some tea, Donna. Are you cold? You're shaking. David, could you grab the afghan off the back of the couch?" I prattled about, trying to make her comfortable. I glanced questioningly at David. He looked pissed – the kind of pissed that for him usually meant he was holding everything else back. David didn't have much use for emotions that required stillness or deep, contemplative thought. He was far better with anger that went hand in hand with action. He stamped off into the living room and returned with the blanket.

"I just don't understand any of this!" Donna whined as I tucked the afghan around her. It was a nice, long cozy one that one of Dad's post-grad students had knitted for him. He joked that must have knitted her notes into it because despite only wielding knitting needles and rarely a pen in his lectures, she managed to earn A's from him every time. I tucked the bulky yarn creation around Donna's shoulders on one end and snaked the other down around her legs. Her feet were icy cold to the touch.

"Is that better?" I asked, pulling a chair up next to her and pouring lukewarm tea in a cup. I was afraid she'd spill and burn herself if I gave her anything hot, she was shaking so hard. David had perched on the stool that sat just inside the kitchen door. It served as a sometime kid's seat at the table, sometime perch for a tired dish washer. It had been painted in varying colors over the years, and was currently currant-red. From his perch he could watch Jon and Jen in the living room, me and his mom in the kitchen, and see out the front window to the driveway and the street.

Donna sniffed and relaxed slightly into the folds of the blanket. "I just don't understand," she whispered. She sounded more like herself as I remembered, the spaced out, self-pitying mess, which wasn't anything I particularly admired, but it was a decided improvement over the screaming banshee Donna who'd gotten out of the car a few minutes ago. I pressed my luck, hoping she might remember something useful while she was in this frame of mind.

"What is it, Donna? What don't you understand?" I asked.

"Anything. What's happening to me? Such a nightmare."

"You've been sick for quite a while. We've all been very worried about you," I told her. What's the last thing you remember?" I asked.

"I've been sick?" she asked. She looked to David for confirmation.

"Yes mom, you've been in the nursing home for a while, ever since your car accident," he supplied. His body language was still tense, but his voice was benign.

"Car accident?" she asked. David and I both nodded.

"Do you remember that?" I asked.

"Today? Stupid van driver! Wouldn't stop." Her voice grew angry for a moment, then faded. "I remember—my room, my bed, looking out my window." She spoke slowly, ponderously. Her shaking was slowing as she warmed up. "I remember nurses, different faces. Some nice, some not nice." Her voice had a sing-songy vibe to it, like someone under a mild hypnosis. I pushed a little further.

"Oh no, not nice? Who was unkind to you?" I asked, leaning forward in my seat.

Donna rocked back and forth in the kitchen chair. I'd given her one of the two at the ends that had the arm rests. I watched her carefully. Her balance wasn't great, I didn't want her falling to the floor.

"Was someone mean to you, mom?" David asked. There was an edge to his voice that I couldn't exactly read. There was an underlying anger there, but I couldn't tell if it was directed at some mean nurse or at his mom. Argh. Donna remained silent, rocking back and forth in the chair.

I reached out to her with my healing gift. Maybe if I could get a look inside her, I could tell what was blocking her memories, or at least if it was magical or medical in nature. I closed my eyes and reached for her, and was blocked.

Boom. Like I'd headfirst run into a brick wall.

I opened my eyes in surprise and rubbed at my forehead. She was unchanged, sitting and rocking, wrapped in the afghan, mumbling quietly. I closed my eyes and reached out again. I felt for the brick wall, tentatively this time. I felt it there, between her mind and mine. I tried reaching out and knocking on it. This time there was a response. A cry of pain from Donna. I pulled back immediately and opened my eyes. David was leaning forward, a thunderous look on his face.

"What are you doing, Angie?" he hissed. "You're hurting her!"

"I'm not, I don't, I can't reach her. Something is

blocking me and when I touched it, she reacted." I didn't know how to explain.

"Whatever it is, it hurt her. You have to stop. Wait for your folks to get back here. Just don't hurt her again! She's been through enough." He choked the last bit out, and then fell silent, his mouth set in an angry line.

The specter of yet another defeat ate at my gut. I felt massively unqualified to figure any of this out. Between Jon's unexplained headaches, my foolish jealousy and attack on Michelle, and my equally foolish attempt to use my healing power for something it wasn't intended to do that hurt Jon instead of helping him. Not to mention the revelation that David's mom might have been behind some of the abuse he endured, and this mysterious, fluctuating lucidity that had landed on her after years of a mostly silent, broken existence. And now this, this whatever it was that was blocking me from even looking at Donna. I had never felt this in over my head. I was so frustrated. I understood none of it. I didn't know what to do or how to fix any of it. Everything I tried was a flop. I was a failure.

Phyllida's final words floated back into my mind; "You must learn to listen, child. Not act. Listen. This is the way to learn."

Well, crap. Okay. I tried to still my mind, to really just listen. I let the moments spin out, not pushing Donna, not reaching out, just waiting. Listening. I heard myself breathing in and out.

I heard Jon and Jen in the living room talking quietly. I couldn't hear the words, but the cadence was familiar. She was asking and he was answering in their twin shorthand. It wasn't code, exactly, but it was a thing they only did with each other, and it wasn't often clear to David or me precisely what was being said.

I heard David's silence. David could do silence like nobody else. Whenever our training games with Mr. Rakow involved anything sneaky, David was King. Nobody could be as silent as he could, and a thought floated through my mind, wondering how he came to be so good at that. I saw it, recognized it, and whooshed it away to think about later. Right now, I was listening.

I heard some traffic outside through the open window, a few cars passed, nobody stopped. The curtain flapped gently against the window frame. I heard the radio crackle from the living room. David got up to respond to it. I heard him identify himself and then my Dad's voice from the other end.

Donna began to speak just then, barely a whisper, her tone sing-songy again. I didn't speak, just listened, focusing entirely on her.

"Lights. Lights in my window. Awake, can't sleep. Can't sleep at night. Too many bad dreams. Lights in my window."

I stayed silent, focusing only on Donna, tuning out the voices in the next room.

"Lady by my bed. Where did you come from, lady? Not a nurse. Terrible dreams." Donna whimpered then, a fearful sound. A childlike sound of night terror.

I knew that sound. I figure everybody does. At least once everyone has that bad dream that you can't quite wake from, the kind of dream where you want to scream, want to run, but you're frozen stiff and all that comes out is that tiny whimper of fear. It was that sound.

I wanted to reach out to Donna, to comfort her. But I didn't. I forced myself to stay still and listen. She was staring out the window, eyes unfocused. I watched her lips move, trying not to miss a word.

"Fire burning, so bright! Black smoke." Donna's lip

curled like she was smelling something bad. "Words, strange words, I don't understand." Donna took a long, shuddery breath. "She's gone. Lights in my window, shining in my EYES!" Suddenly Donna threw back the afghan and pushed her chair backwards away from the table. I recoiled. Her eyes were wide and frightened. Her fingers gripped the arm rests so hard I thought she might tear them right off the chair.

"Open your EYES, Donna!" she growled. "Watch them, DONNA! See where they go! See what they're HIDING! They're keeping SECRETS from you, Donna! Where is it, DONNA?"

My heart was pounding in my chest. She wasn't yelling, far from it. The hissing whisper was barely audible, but she was becoming more agitated by the minute. From the living room I clearly heard, "All clear here. We're going to swing by campus and make sure everything is calm there, then we'll be home. NØGRD out."

"Where is the guardian, DONNA? What are they hiding from YOU??"

"Roger NØGRD. This is NØZCD out."

"G R D" whispered Donna.

Oh crap. "Guys? Guys!"

"G R D! Guard!" Donna stood up from the chair violently, her arms and legs were shaking, her bathrobe hung askew. I stood to block her, to keep her in the kitchen.

From the living room, I heard Jen yelling something to David about grabbing a towel, quick!

"Guys!!"

"GUARDIAN!" Donna screeched. "The Guardian! Campus! Guardian!"

Crap crap crap!!

Donna lunged at me, all hundred and ten pounds of

her, stumbling and raking at my face with ragged finger-nails. I screamed. She scrambled past me, dragging the af-ghan. I tried to run after her and got tangled in it and fell. My weight pulled the blanket free of her staggering figure.

"Guys!" I yelled, struggling to free myself and get up.

"Angie, what? Mom! Wait mom!" David yelled, ago-nized.

"David, stay!" yelled Jen. She sounded scared. Jen never sounded scared. My blood ran cold.

"Angie, grab her! Don't let her go!" David yelled.

I heard tires squeal in the driveway, and the front door banged open.

I staggered into the living room in time to see Jon on the couch in the throes of some kind of seizure, Jen sit-ting next to him, trying to hold his arms down while Da-vid held a hand towel from the bathroom between his teeth, keeping him from biting his tongue. Donna was staggering out the door at an unbelievable pace, given that she was practically dragging one leg and could barely keep her balance. I rushed to catch up to her, and just when I thought I was close enough to catch hold of her bath-robe, she turned and clocked me up under the jaw.

I saw stars and everything got all spinny. The last thing I saw before the lights went out was a green Pontiac four-door in the driveway, and a face I recognized.

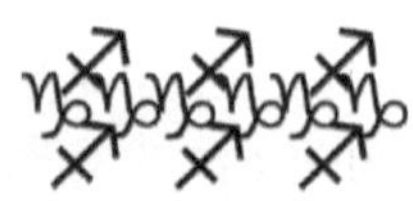

I CAME TO with Barb looking down at me. I scowled and struggled to clear my head. When had Barb gotten here? Last I knew she was off in the desert someplace with Maka and Malinowski, searching for some kind of meteorite that would help with interplanetary communication.

"Angie, breathe. You've had your bell rung, but you'll be fine." I struggled to sit up and the world tilted. "Easy girl. You hit your head on the concrete step."

"Don't push it, Ang. Try to move too fast after that and it's barf city." Malinowski's voice came from somewhere behind me, inside the house. I refrained from turning, it seemed wise.

"Dad! Barb. You have to warn Dad. Donna is on her way to campus. She's with—"

"The librarian. On it, Ang." Barb grinned at me.

"What?" I was so confused. Nobody had been outside with me when I saw Jeanne peel out of the driveway with Donna, half in and half out of the passenger seat, yelling, "Guardian! Campus!"

"Come on, hon," Barb said quietly. "Take a deep breath and let's see if we can move you inside, slowly. If you feel like barfing, hold up a finger and we'll stop."

"But, Dad!"

"I know, Angie." Barb reassured me. "He knows. Jenny and David warned him in time. They're with him now."

"How?" I gasped. The world had settled down but my tummy was warning me to be very, very careful.

"Hush. Try to stand up, you need to be inside."

Slowly, gently, Barb got her arm around me and step by step guided me in the house. She sat me down on the sofa next to Jon who was, amazingly, sitting up and looking less pale and haggard than he had in days. He smiled at me, an almost normal smile. Alesta greeted me with a wet-nosed nuzzle.

They got me settled and Malinowski retrieved a wet

washcloth and a bucket from under the bathroom sink at Barb's direction.

"What is going on?" I demanded, pressing the blessedly cool washcloth to my forehead.

"Let me," said Jon.

"Be my guest," replied Barb.

"Miss Jeanne, the librarian, is a Pilgrim," Jon said. I stared at him. I wasn't sure if it was just because I'd hit my head after being punched out by a crazy lady in a bathrobe, but his eyes seemed a little unfocused. Maybe it was just me.

"Huh?"

"She's a Pilgrim, and a spy. She's been here for years, trying to figure out who the Guardian is so she could find the Portal."

"And she used Donna to figure it out?" I asked, beginning to follow Jon's train of thought.

"She knew Donna was involved in the accident with Mitch, so that's where she started" he said.

"But, why, wait, are you saying Mitch was a Pilgrim too?" I demanded. "And how the heck do you know that?"

"Hang on. Stick with me here." Jon had his arm around my shoulders and he squeezed me. "I need you to follow along because Jen and David are about to need your help.

"I, what?"

Jon squeezed my shoulders again. "Listen."

I shut up and listened.

"Right now, your folks, along with Maka, Jen, David, and Mr. Rakow are on campus setting a trap for Jeanne. They're going to lure her in and trap her, and send her away before she can pass along what she knows to any of the other Pilgrims." Jon spoke slowly enough for me to follow along pretty well.

"How?" I asked.

"They're getting some help from Clara Mills' ghost. She's going to convince Jeanne to try to open the portal herself, before she sends off a message to anybody."

"How do they know she hasn't sent any messages already?" I asked.

"Because that would require her to have this." Malinowski dug something out of his pocket and held it on his open palm. It was a chunk of stone, the likes of which I'd never seen before. It had a layer of some sort of green, crystalline substance running through it. It glowed slightly.

"What's that?"

"It's a chunk of space rock, with special communicative properties," said Barb.

"Which we removed from the glove box of Miss Jeanne's car when it was parked at the mall," gloated Malinowski.

I blinked and started to shake my head, but stopped immediately. That was a bad idea. I hoped more details would be forthcoming and also that I wouldn't need the bucket. "So, Clara is going to lure her in, make her think she can open the Portal, and then what?" I asked.

"Then Lorraine, with your, and Jen and David's help are going to bind her, while your Dad and Maka send her on a one-way trip to a galaxy far, far away." Barb grinned, wolfishly.

"How am I supposed to help with the binding if I'm stuck here and they're all on campus?" I made an ill-advised movement and the spinning started up again. Jon held on to me reassuringly and Malinowski pushed the bucket closer while simultaneously moving himself further away.

"That's where I come in," said Jon.

"How?" I asked, gripping onto my equilibrium with sheer determination. I really, really did not want to barf right now.

"With my exciting new powers that nobody suspected I might have, because apparently, in our family, the only people to exhibit any kind of seeing gifts were the women. I guess nobody figured that a twin might bust that pattern right up."

I stared at him. He was smiling back, but again, something seemed off to me about his eyes. "What?? The headaches? They were your powers coming through? You're a prophet too?" I demanded.

"Not exactly. Maka thinks my powers might be manifesting a little differently than Jen's. And from what we can tell so far, she's right."

"What is it? What can you do?" I asked.

"Here, take my hand, and I'll show you," Jon said holding out the hand that wasn't already around my shoulder.

"What the—"

"It's okay, Honey Bee. You can trust me." Jon whispered and smiled that sweet crooked smile.

A million and one thoughts and feelings rushed me, making my head throb and my stomach flip. Did I? Did I trust Jon? Did I trust him to know how to use powers he'd only possessed for less than an hour, when I was still learning the ins and outs of mine that had manifested years ago? Did I trust him to be in control of some adventure that could save the world, or possibly end it, taking me along for the ride?

I breathed in and out, and I listened. This time I listened to my heart. I put away all my fears and my insecurities, my need to be in control, to be the best, the smartest, the big dang hero. I listened, and was satisfied with the answer I heard.

I put my hand in Jon's and I was transported. For a moment, I could see nothing. Just darkness. Then I could discern little pinpricks of light, like stars in a night sky. And as freaky as that was, I wasn't afraid. I could feel Jon's hand in mine, and I felt completely and totally secure.

"I'm a seer, Maka says, but also something more. Part of problem with the headaches was that other people's feelings and experiences were leaking into my head, and it just sounded like screaming noise until you did whatever you did back there that helped me breathe. That, along with a kind of major seizure, sort of jolted everything into place."

"Oh! Um, yay?" I laughed uncomfortably. "Lucky I tried to kill you so I could have to save you and inadvertently knock your prophetic vision into 20/20?" Ack.

"Okay, let's just get two things straight, here, Ang. Number one, you and I were both hit with a disruptive love spell. Jeanne had it with her, don't you remember? The glitter on the bookmarks?" Jon spoke with surety and disdain for what Jeanne had done. "Michelle got hit with it too," he said, quietly.

"That was a spell? Oh my god!" Then it occurred to me, "Hey! I wonder if I tell mom that I was bespelled if she'll let me off being grounded?" I pondered how best to start *that* conversation.

"Ha! It's worth a shot," Jon replied.

"What's the second thing?" I asked. The pinpricks of light were growing larger and brighter.

"The second thing is that you were trying to help. The spell heightened your feelings, specifically your jealousy, and that monkeyed with your intent some, but still,

Angie, you didn't hurt me. The protection you put on me was strong, and at the same time, my brain was trying to wake up a whole new section of itself, and it needed space to work. You couldn't have known that. None of us could." Jon said.

"So what does it mean? What is this? What can you do?" I asked, feeling somewhat, but not entirely absolved.

"It appears that I can be within the things I see. I can join them, can communicate with them, can know them. People, and objects, too. And I can share it with you, Angie. We can be together this way that goes beyond, so far beyond just *seeing*." Jon's voice was low and calm, fitting comfortably in my head, not just my ears.

I could still sense the pressure of his hand holding mine. My ears were full of the beating of our hearts, a sweet duet. My body was weightless, without footing but still secure. My headache and nausea were blessedly gone. I felt the sensation of movement, but not as if I was moving through air, more like I was the air itself, or rather, we were the air, because we were together in a way I'd never have been able to imagine, and still find difficult to describe.

On the way to our destination, Jon showed me some truths about what had been happening to us the last two days that I don't see how we'd ever been able to know otherwise. He was able to get inside the minds and memories of not only Miss Jeanne, but Michelle, and the van driver from the nursing home. He even showed me one of the women who holed up in the stock room of the store in the mall, but not until after her six-year-old son had been injured by a giant spider Jeanne had conjured up to attack them. He showed me how my dad and Mr. Rakow had agonized over what to tell us after seeing how damaged Donna had been, and what to hold back, both to protect David and also because they knew they had to make Jeanne show her hand so they could find and stop her. He showed me all the chaos Jeanne had wrought, but he also showed me her heart, and what it felt like to be obsessed by the addictive pull of Paradise. It was all awful.

Time, which had seemed to pause while we explored the events of the past days, suddenly fired back up again and a sense of urgency gripped us. Jon turned us away from our explorations and towards our ultimate goal. The pinpricks of light began to blend and grow and form shapes, familiar shapes. Buildings and trees and pathways winding through quiet green spaces. It was the Wesleyan Campus. Then we were there, standing in a spot I knew well, between the Student Center and the smokestack, just behind Old Main.

I turned to look at Jon and found myself instead looking at Mr. Rakow.

"What's going on?" I asked, confused.

Mr. Rakow turned to me and smiled crookedly. Jon's voice in my head said, "We're here. We're sort of, hitching a ride with Mr. Rakow and your mom."

"What?" I looked down at myself, and sure enough. I was my mom. Visions of *Freaky Friday* danced through my head. The one with Jodie Foster, not the remake you're thinking of with Lindsay Lohan. "Oh boy."

"You're telling me!" My mom's voice echoed oddly in my ears.

Oh, yikes. So very much yikes. "Um, so how does this work?" I asked.

"For right now, we need to be here and we can't, so your mom and Mr. Rakow are helping us. This is how it's going to play out. We're going to wait for the signal from Maka telling us that Jeanne is in place. Then you, Jen, and

David are going to activate the power of the Triad and keep her trapped. Then, Lorraine, who is stationed over by Olin hall, will bind her, and your Dad and Maka will do the rest."

"What's the signal?" I asked. Just then a puff of blue smoke appeared over the library.

"That's the signal," said Mr. Rakow/Jon. I turned to look at him and my inner ear protested. I pushed down a wave of nausea. Wow. This was super twisted.

Mom and Mr. Rakow, hands clasped, toting me and Jon on our astral ride-along, moved quickly towards the corner of Old Main. I caught sight of Jen and David approaching from behind the Admin and Science buildings respectively. Then I saw her, Miss Jeanne, walking in an almost trance-like state across the green behind the ghostly figure of Clara Mills. It was the Saturday before Spring Break, so campus was totally deserted except for us. Even so, it was strange to see a ghost floating across campus in broad daylight, just out in the open like it was an everyday occurrence.

We were already positioned in a nearly equilateral triangle, so it was nothing to engage the power of the Triad. I had a brief moment of doubt that this would work, under the circumstances. I felt Jon/Mr. Rakow squeeze my/mom's hand, and I cast my doubt aside and focused on keeping up my point of the trinity.

David's emerald green beam shone brightly and caught Jen's ruby red, I caught them both neatly with my blue beam, only very slightly diminished by the fact that it was a wacky astral projection powered by Jon's spiffy new powers and worn by my mom.

Talk about twisted. This was full goose bozo, as my dad would say.

I felt, rather than heard or saw Lorraine's conjuring.

The area within the triangle thickened as her binding spell began to spill out and fill up the space encompassed by our triangle of power. We continued to stride closer together, reducing the amount of space Lorraine would have to work with, which in turn amplified the power of her spell.

Jeanne felt it too. She threw herself at the hazy form of Clara Mills, who had by then provided a spectral piano upon which to play the music Jeanne believed would open the Portal to Paradise. It was a total scam. While we had to stay close enough to Clara's stomping grounds for her to perform her role in the charade, we were in truth, hundreds of yards away from the actual location of the old C. C. White Music building, on the far side of Old Main, where the real Portal existed.

Clara was nonplussed by Jeanne's theatrics. Jeanne couldn't hurt her and she knew it. Clara laughed a tinkling laugh like the ringing of bells, and slowly disappeared from view accompanied by the ethereal notes of, "Daisy Bell" and her *bicycle built for two* emerging from her phantom piano.

Miss Jeanne wailed, a heartbreaking sound. I felt terrible for her. She'd always been so good to me. Since I was a kid making my Summer Reading visits to pick up my stickers, the library had been my refuge, and Miss Jeanne was always there. I'd gone to her for everything from *Nancy Drew* to *Grimm's* original fairy tales and how to make a macrame plant hanger for my mom. She'd introduced me to Interlibrary Loan, City Directories, and plat maps. She'd helped me with countless school project and had always been so very kind and supportive.

And she'd betrayed me. With the gift of Jon's new sight, I had been able to see all the sneaky moves she'd made. From loading those summer reading bookmarks with a love spell that made Michelle pine after Jon more than ever, and me act more jealous than ever, to selling that potion to Amy and Jill that half poisoned David and wacked out the whole football team. And what she'd done to David's mom was unforgiveable. She'd dosed a sick woman with enough magic to alter her physiology and emotions so much that I didn't know if Donna would ever be able to recover.

The kid that got hurt at the mall would technically recover, but he'd have physical and emotional scars forever, and absolutely none of that mattered to Jeanne. All that mattered to her was that promise of Paradise. We closed in the area of the triangle until we were no more than ten yards apart on each side. The air within was so thick, Jeanne couldn't move, couldn't even scream. Then Maka and my dad stepped in.

With sad and serious eyes, they performed a complicated spell that used another of those weird chunks of space rock as its focus. When they finished, a beam of greenish light pierced the pen in which we'd encased Jeanne, and enveloped her. And then, poof. She was gone. We stood quietly and looked at one another.

There was no congratulatory back slapping after this victory. Instead, we were left with a sense of sadness and duty. Mom was anxious to get to Jeanne's green Pontiac and tend to Donna, so Jon released her and Mr. Rakow from their service as our physical carriers, and she sped off with David to the parking lot. Dad had instructed Barb where to tell the ambulance they could find her as soon as he knew, and they arrived just a few minutes before Mom and David.

Once Jeanne had gone, it released Donna from the spell that was animating her. At that point, she fell back into the barely responsive state she'd existed in for the last four years. Physically though, she was much the worse for wear. The physical exertions Donna had had to make to walk and run, to strike out at Mr. Rakow and me, and to choke the van driver, all of those things had done a number on her body. Her limited abilities became even more limited. She was no longer able to feed herself, and after a week or so, she fell into a semi-coma. The doctors were not optimistic about her condition.

That, as it turned out, had been the bone of contention between my folks. Dad and Mr. Rakow had made the decision not to attempt to break the spell they know Donna was under, in the hopes that she would lead them to the spy. They hadn't told any of us that outright, but the level of understanding between my mom and dad was so great that she'd twigged onto it pretty quickly. There was no way of knowing whether they'd have been successful at breaking the spell, even if they'd tried, and my mom knew that. Breaking someone else's spell, particularly one cast by a magic user of the caliber that Jeanne showed, was a nearly impossible task. But the fact that they decided not to try, even though they understood that it was physically damaging to Donna, was a problem the two of them were going to chew on for a good while.

David had plenty to chew on, too. Jen told me her mom had started looking for a therapist for him. I was sad for him, but glad to hear that there might be help on the way.

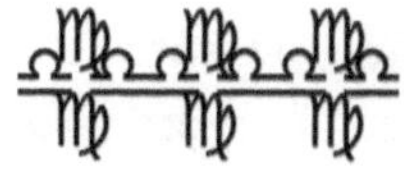

IT WAS ABOUT six weeks later that Jon showed up

for our group movie night wearing his new glasses. He'd chosen big, dorky black plastic frames and I *loved* them. As it turns out, *seeing* isn't all that great for your actual eyeballs. As his power continued to grow, and he continued to practice it under the tutelage of his mom and Maka, his regular everyday eyesight went into rapid decline.

He'd been through two sets of lenses already. By the time the first pair were ready, his vision had deteriorated so much, they'd had to change the prescription. I think everyone around him, including his eye doctor, me, Lorraine and the rest of us were more freaked out by that than Jon was. It really didn't faze him at all. Part of his power meant that he could literally see through anyone's eyes. Anyone. He never had any trouble seeing the chalkboard at school, all he had to do was hitch a ride with someone else and he was good to go. It didn't, he explained, have to be that full-body immersion like we'd done with Mr. Rakow and Mom where we physically had to be on board. Just seeing was more like skimming a stone on the surface of a lake, he said. He could pop in, see what he needed to see, and pop right back out.

The only trouble he had was if nobody else happened to be looking at the exact thing he had in front of him at the moment. Reading in bed and driving were the two big issues there. So, he caved to the necessity of increasingly powerful glasses.

For tonight, he was excited about seeing the movie through his own eyes, and also, he confessed, about seeing my face up close and personal in the dim movie theater light. I didn't argue. We were going to see *Beverly Hills Cop II*, which would almost certainly be not as good as the first one, funny enough to be worth the cost of the popcorn, and in a theater dark enough for some illicit smooching. That made it a trifecta as far as I was concerned.

We were going with a group of kids from school. David had asked out Michelle, and she had said yes. I was surprisingly okay with that. Shortly after our last adventure, I had, of my own volition, gone to Michelle with my pride in my pocket and apologized to her for the body block at her house party. She told me to shove it where the sun didn't shine, and I really couldn't blame her.

It didn't last though. Michelle was, as Jon had said, really a pretty okay person. With some subtle encouragement from him, she managed to forgive me. But only after a week or so of pointed jibes and a few publicly embarrassing episodes to save face. We would never be best friends, but that was all right. At least we were cool.

Jen was also bringing a date. His name was Steve and he was about six inches shorter than her which appeared to bother neither of them in the slightest. Steve was an absolute hoot. He kept everybody laughing no matter if we were going out or just farting around after school. He was amazingly good natured and chill. I found out later that some of that was because of all the weed he was smoking, but a lot of it was just Steve.

Jen drove Clint the Impala. We were to pick up Steve first, and then Michelle. Four of us could share the back seat, the boys occupying the center while Michelle and I claimed the window seats. There was plenty of room back there, so it wasn't a major hardship to share, but elbow room makes for better friends.

En route to Steve's, we talked over some of those things we were only able to discuss amongst ourselves. The hinky stuff.

"Rakow claims those mall spiders were closer to the size of Great Danes than Cocker Spaniels, but Mom just did her smile and nod thing when he said it," Jen was say-ing as she paused Clint the Impala at a Yield sign and looked both ways carefully.

"I wish I'd seen them!" David exclaimed. "Rakow re-fused to let me go inside with him. He said he only had the one machete in the car and I needed to be with Mom." He sighed a little on that last note. Donna had, by that time, fallen into an entirely comatose state. The doc-tors had told us they had no idea how long she might hold on, but to assume she wouldn't come out of it at all this time.

I had told my mom about the nightmares Donna had spoken of, and she and I had very carefully erected a magical dream catcher that hung above her bed. It seemed to be working, or at least the nursing home staff reported that she seemed to be resting more peacefully af-ter we hung it up.

"Rakow said Yardley was amazing inside the mall," Jen continued. "Once they got everybody out, he went in with Rakow to clear the building. He said he didn't want to fire his weapon at the spiders if he didn't have to, be-cause the paperwork on that gets real hairy, and when you're shooting at something that doesn't leave an identi-fiable corpse, the Department asks a lot of questions."

"So, what did he use?" I asked.

"His night stick in one hand, and his Mag Light in the other, Rakow said. Sounds like he was doling out death, Jedi style," Jon replied, laughing.

This was years before we were introduced to the practice of *Jar'kai,* the form of two-handed light saber battle practiced by Darth Maul in the *Star Wars* prequel movies. I remember looking at that on the screen and re-calling this conversation and wondering how far Jon's *see-ing* powers were ranging forward, even back then in the early days.

"Hey, Jon," Jen said. "Steve was asking me when you wanted to jam later. He's really psyched about putting together a band this summer."

"He's pretty amazing on that bass, I didn't know you could do all that with just four strings." Jon said, grinning.

"He's pretty amazing, period," Jen confirmed nodding. The rest of us cracked up, which Jenny imperiously ignored.

"Did you talk to Rakow about using the garage at your mom's for practice?" Jon asked David.

"I did, and he said he thought it was an okay idea as long as we didn't go late at night or act up and piss off the neighbors. We poked around yesterday. We'd need to get in and clean it out some, to make room, but did I tell you we found some drums in there?" David was half turned backwards in the seat, talking to Jon.

"No! Cool!"

"Yeah, I don't know who left them, I don't remember Mitch ever having them so it must have been before that. It's not a whole trap set or anything, but there's a snare and a couple of big bongo things. Plus, a box of little stuff, like tambourines and that thing with the ridges that you play with a stick. What did Señora Bird call that gourd thing the dude brought to class last month, Ang?"

"A güiro?" I supplied, from my vast trove of useless knowledge.

"Yeah! That thing!" David crowed.

"I'm having a vision," I announced. Jen and Jon stared at me quizzically.

"For real?" Jen asked.

"No, just stick with me here," I replied, crossing my legs yogi-style and closing my eyes. "I see the four of us, plus Steve forming a punk/folk/rock band and traveling the contiguous 48 states in Clint, the Impala, battling monsters and saving the world between gigs," I intoned.

"Cool! What about Michelle?" David asked.

"I see groupies galore," I went on, doing my best imitation of Johnny Carson's, *Carnac the Magnificient.*

"Cool!" David bounced in his seat.

"We'll be offered contract after contract by the big recording companies, and we'll turn them all down, preferring to stay underground and independent, so we can continue our secret lives as magical do-gooders, rescuing people in distress and puppies along the way," I went on.

"Ooh! Puppies!" David said, grinning. "Go on, Angie!"

"They'll call us," I paused, "Undercover Seer and the Punk Cusp Kids".

"Oh, that's terrible," Jon laughed.

The silliness continued after we'd picked up Steve and Michelle. We made it to the mall in time for a stroll past the stores, two of which advertised new, improved security measures in the event of wild animal or other criminal incursions. The record store, on the other hand, was advertising a summer open mic contest for local bands, to be held outside in the parking lot. The boys swarmed around the sign, scrambling to sign us up.

Jen and I hung back, watching.

"I've been wondering what the oboe would sound like, hooked up to an amp," I confessed to Jen.

"I suppose I could play the tambourine," Jen mused.

"Do you suppose any of these dreams might stand a chance? Or are we doomed to a life of duty and tragically hinky adventure?" I asked, staring across at the book store display of teen books, and thinking sadly about Miss Jeanne.

Jen pulled her car keys out of her pocket which hung

on a Magic 8-ball key chain I'd found for her at Things-ville. She shook it, and we both stared expectantly as the little words appeared in the window.

"Reply hazy, try again."

We looked at each other and shrugged. The boys and Michelle piled over and we headed into the theater, tick-ets in hand, hope in our hearts and uncertainty on the horizon.

Tales of the Zodiac Cusp Kids

Available from Snowy Wings Publishing

Something Wicked
the First Tale of the Zodiac Cusp Kids

It's 1983. Angie, Jenny, and David are watching MTV, riding bikes, and looking forward to summer vacation before they start junior high school. Lincoln, Nebraska is a pretty quiet place to grow up, and when the kids take off at 5:00 am to deliver newspapers on Jenny's route, they aren't expecting trouble. So, when a creature straight out of a horror movie appears, the kids are forced to draw on their wits, their strengths, and most of all their friendship to survive.

Something Haunted
the Second Tale of the Zodiac Cusp Kids

The summer of 1983 is over. After weeks of healing from their first adventure and some specialized basic training with Mr. Rakow, Angie, Jenny and David are feeling prepared for the horrors junior high will surely bring. The final weekend of vacation, a bizarre tornado tears through Lincoln, upending gravestones and depositing supernatural debris on the school grounds. The gang has their hands full with the demands of starting junior high on top of trying to figure out an otherworldly mystery, and their friendship begins to feel the strain. But the malevolent ghost haunting the school is ramping up its attacks on students, and the kids are going to have to get it together in time to save the school.

Something Lost
the Third Tale of the Zodiac Cusp Kids

It's a Friday afternoon in the spring of 1985, when Crystal and Barb, two girls from Whitehall, the neighborhood group home for troubled kids, approach Angie at school. Crystal's little sister has disappeared, and her foster parents and the police think she's just another runaway. Crystal doesn't believe it, and when she and Barb learn there's a ghost involved, they know they're going to need the kind of help Angie, David and Jenny have developed a reputation for.

The Zodiac Cusp Kids enlist some extra help from Jen's twin Jon and a couple of very special German Shepherd pups to uncover what has really happened to Crystal's sister, and what they find is darker and more complex than anyone imagined.

Something Found
the Fourth Tale of the Zodiac Cusp Kids

Just over a week has passed since Angie, David and Jenny said goodbye to Barb and Alesta, the German Shepherd pup when David and Jenny convince Jon and Angie to come to a dance at the neighborhood Rec

Center. Mysterious things begin to appear as soon as the girls start getting ready for the dance. Jenny's prophecies guide them to a magical artifact that transports the Zodiac Cusp Kids away from the dance on a world-hopping rescue that opens their eyes to a terrifying new enemy, and to some powerful magical allies closer to home than they'd dreamed.

Something Found is the fourth of seven stories drawn from Angie's diaries. Kept safely hidden for decades, they tell how the kids spent their teenage years – working with their mentor, Mr. Rakow, and Jenny's mom, Lorraine, who dabbles in witchcraft, to realize their power and battle the forces of darkness that menace their hometown.

Something Twisted
the Fifth Tale of the Zodiac Cusp Kids

Two years have passed since Angie, David, and Jenny returned from their star-hopping adventure and learned the identity of the Guardian. Now sophomores in high school, the kids are trying to juggle saving their hometown while also having social lives, playing on sports teams, acting in plays, and studying healing magic outside of class. When those worlds begin to collide with dangerous magic, the kids have their hands full figuring out who to trust. Then, David's mom gets dragged into the mess and the Guardian puts his relationship with the whole team on the line to discover the identity of the culprit. Plus, Great Dane-sized-spiders. Hold onto your hats, Something Twisted is going on!

Something Fatal
the Sixth Tale of the Zodiac Cusp Kids

Coming June 1, 2021

Something Final
the Last Tale of the Zodiac Cusp Kids

Coming September 7, 2021

About the Author

Sarah Dale is an author, mom, partner, daughter, step-mom, friend, dog-walker, cat-appreciator, library book-balancer, word lover, think-thinker and picture-taker living in Lincoln, Nebraska, and just generally trying to get things done.

www.sarahdaleauthor.com

Facebook: facebook.com/wecouldbeheroesnovel/

Twitter: @sarahdaleauthor

Instagram: instagram.com/wecouldbeheroesnovel/
Goodreads: goodreads.com/stillphoenix

Amazon: amazon.com/author/stillphoenix

Other titles you might enjoy from Snowy Wings Publishing

Sand and Snow
-Janina Franck

Diamond Mage
-Dorothy Dreyer

Tracker220
-Jamie Krakover

Look for these and more at
www.snowywingspublishing.com/books

www.ingramcontent.com/pod-product-compliance
Lightning Source LLC
Chambersburg PA
CBHW031631200726
48288CB00019B/1297